To

G000138841

Enjoy

Dave Floyd

MUST FLEA

A MADS & LYNDSEY MYSTERY

D S FLOYD

BLACK SHEEP

First Published 2017 by Black Sheep Design

ISBN 978-1-898735-02-1

Black Sheep Design
info@bsdpub.com

Dedicated to Carol Townend

*The first person to make
me believe I could write well.*

Acknowledgements

Thanks to Andrew Chapman, Kez Floyd, Claire Harris, Sue Horlock and Corin Telfer, who read early versions of this novel and provided me with useful feedback.

Thanks also to Marie Clement whose editing advice was invaluable.

Finally, thanks to the Kingston crew: Adam, Aless, Carlo, Chidi, Chris, Isabel, Jaclyn, Julia, Luke, Stephen, Tamara and Tamsin whose detailed critiquing helped improve the finished article no end.

'Damn Barry!' If not for that cheating hound, she could be tucked up nice and cosy in bed. Instead, she was leaving her grandad's house at five in the morning to set up and run his market stall in lieu of rent she couldn't afford to pay.

Lyndsey closed the front door behind her and strode towards the small van parked on the driveway. The temperature was mild for October, but the summer had continued so far into autumn this year, it felt chilly by comparison. She glanced up, expecting the forecasted heavy clouds, but breathed a sigh of relief on realising the forecast must have been wrong.

Five minutes later, she reached the huge market area that had once been derelict factories and warehouses to the south of Brentford High Street. She manoeuvred her way through the gates and nosed her way along the single lane track past other traders busy setting up their stalls. Only the meagre lighting for each stall provided any illumination other than her headlights as they cut through the gloom. She drove into the alcove to her pitch and parked at the back, next to the van owned by the trader behind.

She turned off the engine, rested her arms on the steering wheel and lay her head on them. The desire to return home was tempting, but she would be damned if she would give Barry the satisfaction of thinking she was avoiding him.

'Come on, Lynds. You can do this!'

After a couple of deep breaths, she arranged her chestnut hair into a ponytail and climbed out.

She lowered the stall fronts and secured the legs before starting to unload the merchandise. Two years had passed since she last helped Grandad and she swore the items looked the same as before. First, she laid out some old books of postcards and cigarette cards and positioned them right centre. To the left went two wooden boxes of old Brentford programmes that she struggled to lift. Next, four ornamental knives dating back to either the Boer or Great wars (depending on which Grandad sensed the prospective buyer would be most interested in). She filled up the edges and back with assorted old clocks and barometers, each of which would 'only need a small amount of attention' for them to work like new.

She ducked beneath the table top to check the display from the front, made a few final adjustments, before ducking back again and searching the van for any stray items. After closing the back doors, she scanned the market as other traders bustled about, setting up their stalls.

Barry occupied the stall across from hers and so far there was no sign of him. She hoped he had dropped dead to avoid the inevitable meeting, then scolded herself for the thought.

She had been helping out here three years ago when she first met Barry. A lump surged in her chest as she thought of him, but before she could decide whether anger or self-pity was behind it, Bob's voice shook her from her reverie.

'Lynds! Alright, darlin'? What are you doing here? Hey, Jools, look who's back.'

Lyndsey turned and smiled as Bob approached. His short, dark brown hair was cut in a side parting and salt and peppered on the sides. A thick blue woollen jumper and a red and black puffa jacket accentuated his plump body. In contrast, his drainpipe jeans resembled bird legs sticking out the bottom. Due to the extra weight filling out his face, he passed for mid-forties rather than his real age of fifty-eight.

Lyndsey found herself engulfed in a huge bear hug. Bob ran the mirror stall on the next pitch along with his wife, Jools. No sooner did he release her than she was embraced in another one.

'Hello love. How are you? Bert's OK, isn't he?'

'Hi, Bob. Hi, Jools. Yes, Grandad's fine. I needed to move back in with him, so he roped me into doing the stall at weekends.'

Jools laughed. 'Wily old dog, he is. Bet he's pleased as punch you're back but figured he could take advantage while he has the chance.'

'I'm sure you're right, but I'm not in a position to argue. At least it gives me the opportunity to catch up with the pair of you. How are you both? You're looking well'

Jools' shoulder length hair was losing its battle with the onslaught of grey but still displayed enough colour to remind Lyndsey of her once fiery red mane. She had also put on a couple of kilos, but she worked out and kept as trim as she could. She wore a maroon sweatshirt and a cream, hip length coat somewhat more flattering than Bob's, and her jeans-clad legs appeared more in proportion than her husband's. She looked more her age than Bob, but only a brave or foolhardy person would mention that within her earshot.

'So hang on,' said Bob. 'Why did you need to move

back? I thought you lived in Barry's flat in Hounslow?'

They all involuntarily turned their heads towards Barry's empty pitch.

'Yes, but the newspaper laid me off. When I got home earlier than expected, I found him in bed with some other woman.'

'You're joking! If you want me to have a word with him, Lynds, just say.'

'Thanks, Bob, but as satisfying as it would be watching you give him a beating, he's not worth getting arrested over.'

'Oh, sweetheart.' Jools moved in for another hug. 'Never you mind, everything will sort itself out. I always said you were too good for him, didn't I Bob?'

'You did, love. Don't you worry, Lynds. He never deserved you, and in a week or two you'll wonder why you put up with him for as long as you did.'

'Speak of the devil,' said Jools. Barry guided his estate into the alcove. What looked like a cupboard poked out the back of the car, its rear door crudely tied down with rope. Rather than park at the back of his pitch, he turned and backed up to the furniture stall at the end.

Lyndsey tore her eyes away and turned to Bob and Jools.

'Hey, I'm all set up. Can I give you a hand?'

'Of course,' said Bob. 'Tell you what, you climb in and hand the mirrors out to us while we arrange them. How does that sound?'

Bob's suggestion sounded perfect, and she clambered into the back of his van. Once everything was displayed, Lyndsey climbed out and glanced across the alcove.

'What's with the tent across the way?'

'That's Mary,' said Jools. 'She's a local artist, as you can guess from the paintings. Shares the pitch with Martin who sells second-hand books. They seem nice enough, keep themselves to themselves.'

'It looks odd, just half a stall protected by an open-front tent.'

'We thought that at first, but I suppose it must be easier to cover a few boxes with a plastic sheet than the paintings.'

'What happened to Gloria and her lamps?'

'She died, poor love. One week she was there, next she was gone. None of us even knew she was sick. I don't think she wanted the fuss. Inoperable brain tumour, so Rhonda at the end told us.'

'Oh, what a shame. Gloria was such a character.'

'Yes, she was. She was quieter than usual during her last few weeks, but we didn't think anything of it. Or maybe that only occurred to us after the event. Hindsight can play tricks with the memory, don't you think?'

'I suppose so. Always twenty-twenty, as they say. I must go back to my stall. I don't want to disappoint the hordes when the gates open, do I?'

Jools laughed as Lyndsey smiled and rolled her eyes. The time was almost 6.30, opening time, though it never livened up before 7.30, or even later when it rained.

Stallholders from other parts of the market armed with torches darted from stall to stall, flitting over the products on offer for items they could strike a deal for and sell at a profit to the weekday regulars at their shops. The speed of their browsing was the obvious factor that differentiated the dealers from regular customers.

Barry aside, she found it comforting that the majority of the faces she remembered were the same as before. She nodded and said 'hello' to Ranjit whose eye-catching array of bright coloured fabrics and clothing often attracted people in to browse their little enclave. Unlike his materials, he always appeared understated. This morning he wore an old brown suit over a black polo neck jumper.

His was one of the few stalls with a permanent roof as he rented the pitch seven days a week so didn't need to take it down for someone else to use the stall on weekdays.

Most other weekenders used temporary covers or made do with plastic sheets to protect their merchandise from the rain.

When the market had been conceived, the initial plans included permanent roof structures, but some potential stallholders objected as they meant they wouldn't be able to park their vans behind the pitches. Never slow on the uptake when it came to saving money, the Council considered the objections and—in a move only the only the most naïve found surprising—ruled they had merit. Consequently, the potential to erect cover remained, but individual stallholders decided whether to take advantage of it or not.

To her right were Bob and Jools with their mirrors. Since Lyndsey's parents died in a car crash fifteen years earlier, they had fussed over her and treated her like the daughter they never had.

To their right, Bill and Rhonda ran a second-hand furniture stall that closed off the back of the enclave. In their late forties, they originated from South Wales. Bill wore a black beanie hat to protect his shaved head from the elements and a donkey jacket. Rhonda, as always, looked immaculate, as if gracing a fifties Hollywood set. Her light brown hair cascaded over her shoulders without a single hair daring to fall out of place. The 'scruffy work clothes' she wore to the market fitted just a little too well to think she didn't take as much effort in dressing down as most people did when dressing up. The furniture they brought to the markets was the excess they picked up from house clearances, the more expensive antique items being set aside for sale from their shop in nearby Richmond.

Next was Mary's tent. Off-white with back and sides as well as a roof, not dissimilar to something one might expect in a movie based in a desert. Mary sat just inside the entrance reading a book. Her dyed black hair was fashioned in a spiked, pixie cut with a shock of scarlet to the front left side. Heavy eye make-up vied with her hair for attention, stark against her pale skin. She wore a body hugging leather jacket, black skinny jeans and a pair of black, winklepicker ankle boots with what appeared to be skull buckles. The paintings she displayed exploded with bright, bold colours, contrasted against black or purple backgrounds. Pastoral scenes seemed not to be Mary's forte.

Sat with his back to the tent and also reading was Martin. Although he looked to be in his early to mid-thirties, his clothing choices comprised an old band sweatshirt, jeans and trainers. With his dishevelled hair escaping from his side-parting and his black, plastic framed glasses, he looked every bit the first year university student.

Next along was Barry, who sold records and CDs

alongside t-shirts and sweatshirts printed with band designs. The mainstay of his trade was rock and punk and Green Day played through his sound system, noticeable enough to attract attention while not so loud as to make the other stallholders in the vicinity complain. Lyndsey saw Barry looking across and jerked her head away, not wanting him to think she was staring at him. From the corner of her eye, she saw him smirk. He ducked down, making his way out.

Damn. He caught me looking.

Lyndsey kept her head facing the final stall run by a man named Sammy. He stood over six feet tall with a solid build effortlessly filling his extra-large hoodie. His ebony skin tone made him almost disappear into the spacious hood until he flashed one of his dazzling smiles, something of a regular occurrence. He sold a gruesome mix of stuffed animal heads and mounted skulls. He always claimed they died natural deaths instead of being the proceeds of hunting, but she doubted he checked too fastidiously. Then again, there was the possibility her vegan Spidey-senses were being too touchy, making her distrustful. Lyndsey couldn't help but like him, regardless. His frequent smiling and easy-going demeanour were hard to dislike.

Barry swaggered across and, as he approached her stall, she turned her head to face him.

'Well, Lynds, I'm sure you miss me but I didn't expect you to manufacture a meeting quite so soon.'

'Barry, the only thing I'd regret missing you with would be something heavy. Go away.'

'You don't mean that. If you want to come back, just ask. Don't hang about, though. I'll only be free for a small time.'

'I can assure you, my mind will always link you and the word small. I assume the girl I caught you with last week had more sense than I did and scampered off as fast as her slender legs would carry her?'

'Candy? That was never serious. We got chatting in a record shop and had an afternoon to kill so figured on having some fun. You're overreacting, Babe. You should take it as a compliment I'd rather be with you than her, and I wouldn't know that without conducting a test run, now would I?'

Lyndsey wondered for a moment how hard she could hit him with a broken barometer, but took a couple of deep breaths and resisted the temptation.

'Candy? Did you cheat on me with someone called Candy? Oh wait, please don't tell me she was Kandy with a "K".'

'I'm not sure. It might be Kandi with a "K" and an "I" for all I care. To be honest, I didn't ask her to spell her name out for me.'

He smirked again, knowing he was getting under her skin. She wanted to scream and launch herself at him like a banshee, but refused to give him the satisfaction. She felt relieved when between the scurrying dealers with their torches, someone walked up to his stall and stood there waiting.

'You have a customer by the looks of things, Barry. Go away and leave me alone. Now.'

He glanced over his shoulder and saw a silhouette in the subdued lighting that enabled the market to open before sunrise during the winter months. He turned back and gave her a final smirk.

'Well, don't forget, you're welcome to come crawling back but don't take too long. I won't wait forever.' He winked and strolled back across the concrete.

Lyndsey glared after him. How she wished she could morph into a video game end of level boss. She would burn two holes through his body from the fire in her eyes. But wishes weren't horses, as her grandad always used to tell her, and Barry kept walking unencumbered by laser burns of any description. She was surprised to feel her hands shaking and balled them into fists in an attempt to stop, or at least to prevent anyone noticing. Tears of anger burnt hot in the corners of her eyes, and she wiped her sleeve across them.

She wondered what she had seen in him. His one-time roguish smile seemed more like a leer this morning. The walk that once screamed confidence now came across as arrogance. Sure, in the right light he looked like a budget Brad Pitt, and he was ridiculously charming when he chose to be. But had he managed to keep up the act for the last three years or had she just ignored any slips? She had always felt guilty for working silly hours at the paper and might have blamed that for any occasional mood swings he had displayed. Had the loss of her once best friend, Mads, to marriage three years ago made her settle?

What was I thinking?

Bob slid his arm around her shoulders, shaking her from her reverie.

'Don't let him needle you, love. He isn't worth the energy. Here, take this and buy Jools and I a breakfast roll and cup of coffee each, plus whatever you want for yourself. Go on, the walk to the catering van will calm you down a bit.'

She took the offered twenty pound note.

'Grr, I just ... I try not to but can't help myself.'

'Take the high ground. The more Barry sees he's having an effect, the more he'll be encouraged to continue. Take a break and buy some food. We'll keep an eye on your stall, though I don't imagine many will turn up yet.'

He squeezed her shoulders and let her go.

'Thanks, Bob. Two breakfast rolls and coffees? No sugar, right?'

'Them's the ones, and whatever you want. If you come back with nothing for yourself, I won't be happy— and you don't want to see me when I'm angry.'

He smiled at her, and she laughed in response. In all the years she had known him, Bob had never got angry once, at least not with her. He was like a big teddy bear who always had her back.

'Well, I doubt there'll be much I'll eat, but I'll try my best, OK?'

'That's the spirit. Oh, while I think of it, did you enjoy your birthday the other week?'

She studied him and furrowed her brow. 'My birthday's not until December. You know that, right? Or does Jools do all the present buying in your house?'

'Ah, busted. Sorry, my bad. Maybe I confused you with someone else. Blame it on the starvation ... hey, haven't you gone to the van yet?'

Lyndsey raised an eyebrow, not convinced, but ducked under the stall before aiming one final glare in Barry's direction. The person she thought to be a customer was having an animated, if hushed, argument with him, and he appeared even bigger closer up.

With any luck, he'll punch him.

The walk calmed her down a little. As she joined the short queue, Lyndsey set about quelling the remainder of her anger. Bob had a point. If she refused to react, Barry will get bored and move on. Even if he didn't, he wasn't worth wasting all this emotional energy. He was part of her past. She needed to put him behind her and write the whole thing off to experience.

She chuckled as she remembered the horrified expression on Bob's face when he admitted not knowing her birthday. That was strange, though. She couldn't imagine why he thought it had passed, even if he didn't remember the actual date. Before long she found herself at the head of the queue.

'Hey, vegan girl, not seen you in ages. How's it hanging?'

Madge had been running the catering truck since the

market had opened almost five years earlier. She was a Jamaican woman in her early sixties who displayed her graveyard grin every time she smiled.

'Not so much hanging as drooping forlornly, but I'll survive. How are you?'

'Same old, same old. So what can I get you? The jacket potatoes aren't ready yet, but I can do you a baked bean toastie.'

'Sounds lovely. A black tea with that and a couple of breakfast rolls and two white coffees without sugar too, please.'

'No problem, love. It'll be a few minutes, OK?'

'That'll be fine, and if you can rustle me up something I can carry everything back on, that would be grand.'

'I'm sure I can find you something.' Madge gave the scribbled order to one of the catering elves behind her and asking the person behind Lyndsey what they wanted.

Five minutes later, Madge handed her the food and drinks in a box top.

'Thirteen-fifty, please love.'

Lyndsey gave her the twenty pound note and waited for the change which she dropped into the box top to return to Bob.

'Thanks, Madge. See you tomorrow.'

'OK, love. Take care of yourself.'

Lyndsey smiled at her and strolled back. When she arrived, Barry's visitor had gone, and Barry also appeared to be missing. She ambled across to the mirror stall. They didn't bother with the front table flaps as it was easier to display mirrors on the ground and use artist's easels for a double layer effect.

'Here you go. Two coffees, two breakfast rolls,' said Lyndsey, pointing the items out. 'And there's your change.'

'You keep hold of that,' said Bob. 'It isn't much but might help tide you over until your benefits kick in.'

'Don't be silly. I still have most of my last pay cheque.'

'Well, that won't last long, I'm sure. I mean it. Think of it as an unbirthday present. It's the least I can do after giving you an extra birthday. Go on, before Jools grabs it.'

He winked conspiratorially.

'Yes, you do what he says. Lucky she's deaf, else she might have heard him,' said Jools, as she strolled across with a wry smile on her face to take one of the coffees from the lid. She drew up a chair to act as a makeshift table. 'Here you go, Lynds.'

'Lyndsey put the tray down and, after a brief pause, pocketed the change.

'Thanks.'

'Don't you worry about it,' said Jools. 'What's this about extra birthdays? I want one of those, as long as the numbers don't accumulate on my age.'

'Oh, nothing,' said Bob. 'I think I got confused with someone else. For some reason, I thought her birthday was a couple of weeks ago.'

'Why would you think that? You know her birthday's near Christmas.'

'Yes, going prematurely senile, I guess. Can we stop concentrating on my stupidity and eat?'

They both set about their rolls and fell silent. Lyndsey nibbled at her toastie, knowing from experience that its innards would be searing and capable of removing several layers of skin if she wasn't careful. She eventually broke through without suffering injury and squeezed the gap in the bread open a little, blowing into it to allow the steam to escape through the spout-like hole.

Jools took a sip of coffee. 'I don't buy that,' she said. 'You're well aware of when Lyndsey's birthday is. Why would you think it was weeks ago?'

'Oh for goodness sakes, woman. Let it drop. Aren't I allowed to make a mistake once in a while without getting your permission first?'

Lyndsey smiled to herself as the familiar sound of Bob and Jools playfully bickering amongst themselves brought back memories.

'Of course, my dear. You make mistakes on a day to

day basis and never fly them by me first, else I would help you avoid them. But I don't understand how you would make that one. You've never once forgotten her birthday. Mine, yes. Even your own sometimes, but not Lyndsey's.'

Bob sighed. 'Well, I suppose there must be a first time for everything. So Lynds, what happened at the paper? I thought things were going well.'

Lyndsey shrugged. 'There isn't much call for actual local reporting nowadays. Most event organisers write their own articles and an intern can copy and paste as well as I can.'

'There are times I hate the way the world is changing. Everything's about profit, while people are expendable. So what are you looking to do for a job now?'

'I'm not sure. There isn't much about so I can't afford to be too fussy. Unless I want to work on the stall every weekend.'

'Don't you mind that. Take some time to think about what you want to do. Believe me; you're way too smart for your dreams to be crushed by the drudgery of a dead-end job you hate. Better to take a bit of time and wait for something you'll enjoy.'

'Bob's right,' said Jools with a smile, prompting a feigned expression of shock from Bob. 'Oh for that advice before I married him. Imagine what heights I might have scaled without him weighing me down like an anchor.'

'Haha, you'd be lost without me, as you well know. If not for me, who would make you feel so superior.'

'Trust me, my dear. Boneheaded men aren't in short supply. It just happened I was looking for one with a sense of humour, and you stumbled along at the right moment.'

She popped the last of her roll into her mouth and gave Bob a peck on the cheek.

'I'm going to sit in the van where I'll be warmer and tally up last week's books until the sun deigns to appear. Catch you later Lynds. You have a customer waiting. Quick, before he escapes.'

Lyndsey saw a man browsing her stall.

'OK guys, better go. Thanks for breakfast.'

'You're welcome.'

She picked up her tea and edged her way through the narrow walkway between the mirrors, still gingerly holding the toastie that, as yet, showed no signs of cooling down.

Lyndsey sat down as the man flicked through the programmes. Every so often he took one out of the box and studied it through its protective plastic bag, then put it back. She continued to nibble on the toastie until it cooled enough to eat. She hadn't realised how hungry she was until she visited the catering truck. She polished it off and washed it down with the remainder of the tea.

The lights behind her clicked off as the sensors cut out in response to the sun's arrival. She sat and watched other stalls' lights turn off, not together, but in a random fashion like twinkling fairytale stars. As the weak autumn sun rose, people began to show up and milled around in small herds. In another hour or so the marketplace would be bustling and lively.

The thought occurred to her that Barry was still missing and she wondered where he was. He rarely disappeared for long once the gates opened. She shrugged and pulled an e-reader from her pocket to while away the time until another potential customer appeared.

A few minutes later the music stopped, and she glanced up from her book again. This was strange. As infuriating as he was, Barry should have returned by now, and his absence piqued her curiosity. She put the reader back in her pocket and stood to get a better view.

Nothing appeared out of the ordinary. A couple who Lyndsey guessed to be in their early forties were admiring a mirror and she heard Jools trying to cajole them in with, 'Lovely, isn't it? I always say a house isn't a home without mirrors.' Across from there a teenage goth girl, who she assumed was their daughter, studied one of Mary's more startling creations. An older couple were browsing a dressing table at the end, but no sign of Barry.

Unbelievable! He is as annoying when he isn't to be found as when he is.

As she gazed across at the furniture, she realised she recognised something.

That's what he had in his car this morning!

'Cheeky git,' she muttered, as she ducked beneath the stall and strode across to Bill who was taking some smaller items from his lorry.

'Bill, did Barry give you that wardrobe this morning?'

'Hello, Lyndsey love. Yes, he said to get what I could and split the money with him.'

'I bet he did. It's my bloody wardrobe! I left it at his flat when I moved out last week.'

'Oh.' He stared down at his feet and shuffled them for a moment. 'Do you want it back? I can mark it sold so you can take it with you later if you like?'

Lyndsey looked around, hoping to see Barry so she could give him a piece of her mind.

'No, but if you sell it, I want his share of the money. Fair enough? You don't need to take my word the wardrobe's mine, ask him when he reappears.'

'Of course, I had no idea. How are you keeping, love? I haven't seen you here for ages.'

'I've had better weeks, to be honest.' She paused. 'I'm

sorry I leapt down your throat. It came as a shock when I recognised my wardrobe.'

'Don't mention it. I hope things start looking up for you.'

'Thanks, you and Rhonda doing well?'

'Can't complain, but if I don't finish emptying the lorry, she'll be on my case soon enough.'

'I'll let you crack on. Make sure you get a good price, OK?'

He winked, and she walked back, still fuming inside.

Wait until I get my hands on Barry, I'll bloody kill him!

As she sat down again, a man strolled up to the stall. He was somewhat overdressed in a hat, coat and scarf considering the mildness of the weather. From the little she could see of him, Lyndsey reckoned he might be in his mid-fifties or so.

'Hi,' he said. 'You might be interested in these.'

He handed her a box, which she opened to find it full of photos.

'Can you leave them with me I'll ask my grandad how much he'll offer for them tonight. How does that sound? If you come back tomorrow, I can either pay you, or you can take them back.'

'No, you misunderstand me. I don't want anything for the photographs and wouldn't expect you to sell them. I literally meant YOU might be interested. You are Lyndsey Marshall?'

She paused for a moment, surprised to hear him speak her name.

'Do I know you? Sorry if I do, I can't place you.'

He smiled. 'No, you don't, but I knew your parents. I attended their funeral and slipped away afterwards, so I can't think of any reason you'd remember me. The pictures are of them, so I thought you would like them.'

'Oh ....' She stared down at the box and was about to ask how he knew she would be working at the market when a piercing scream sounded from the furniture stall.

She craned her neck to see what had happened but Bill, Rhonda and the couple who had been browsing obscured her view. She turned towards the man again, but he had disappeared while her attention had been elsewhere.

I don't believe it. This morning couldn't be any weirder if it tried.

She replaced the lid on the photos and stashed them on the front seat of the van, before dashing over to find out what the kerfuffle had been about.

She was only halfway across when she stopped. One of the day's mysteries was solved, at least. Barry lay on the ground. Dead, if his awkward position and glassy-eyed stare were anything to go by. He must have tumbled out when someone opened her wardrobe door. She breathed in and raised her hands to her mouth in shock, not breathing out again for what seemed to her like minutes.

'Come on, love. You don't need to be looking at that.'

She felt an arm around her shoulders and allowed Bob to guide her to the mirror stall. Jools cleared the seat, and they sat her down. She tried to talk, but the only sound to emerge was a squeak.

'Shh, you sit quiet for a bit while Bob goes and gets you some tea. You'll be OK once the shock passes.'

She slumped against the back of the chair, numb. For all Barry's faults, and annoying as he was, she couldn't imagine anyone would go as far as to kill him.

A few minutes later, Bob returned with some black tea. She took the cup from him and cradled it in her hands, staring at what was going on without taking much in. The police had cordoned off Bill and Rhonda's furniture stall and had begun to erect a tent around the area where Barry still lay in front of the open wardrobe. They were now moving back the crowd to cordon the alcove off.

Only when halfway down did she realise the tea contained sugar. Ugh, she thought, but carried on drinking until there was about a centimetre left before placing the cup under the chair. Refreshed, she stood to join Bob and Jools who were speaking to each other in hushed tones.

'Word travelled fast,' she said, staring back at the rubberneckers who had congregated behind the police tape.

'That it did,' said Jools. 'Are you sure you're OK? That must have been a shock for you.'

'Yes, I think so. I just needed a sit down to steady my nerves a bit. Thanks for the tea.'

'No worries,' said Bob. 'We were wondering who killed him. It wasn't us, though I was planning on having a word or three with him when he reappeared.'

'And you had nothing to do with it,' added Jools. 'You were at the food trailer.'

Lyndsey paused a moment. 'What were you going to talk to him about, Bob?'

'Don't you worry about that,' he said. 'I didn't, that's all you need to know.'

'Well, what about the big bloke who was arguing with him when I went for breakfast? I'm not sure what his problem was but from his body language, Barry had wound him up somehow.'

Bob and Jools looked at each other. 'I don't remember anyone, do you, Bob?'

'Nor me. Barry was giving Lyndsey a hard time so I made my way to her stall to tell him to do one, but he wandered away before I got the chance. With the other traders darting in and out you kind of zone people out unless they're browsing your pitch. Who was this guy, Lynds?'

'I'm not sure. I told Barry he had a customer, that's what got him away from me, but I didn't catch his face.

He walked up to the stall and stood there waiting. I'm sure I would recognise his gait again, but can't think of any other specific features I could pick out. He was a big built guy and judging by his stance, more muscle than fat, but I imagine that covers more than a few men in West London.'

Minutes turned to hours and the time reached ten o'clock by the time an ambulance edged its way through the crowd at the end. The police lowered the cordon to allow access and it backed its way between the stalls and stopped in front of the furniture stall tape. Two paramedics climbed out and opened the back doors to retrieve a stretcher that they took into the tent. A couple of minutes later they came back out carrying Barry's bagged body. They put it into the ambulance and drove away.

A man who Lyndsey took to be a detective emerged holding a plastic bag. He held it in the air and barked, 'Does anyone recognise this knife?'

She stared with horror, and everybody else stood gaping at her. She glanced across at her stall where three knives lay on the tabletop. Yes, she recognised the knife, as did everyone gawking at her. It was one of hers.

The inspector handed the bagged knife to one of the officers and walked towards Lyndsey. She sat down, wishing the ground would open up and swallow her as his measured steps took an age to reach her.

He wore a taupe raincoat over a dishevelled, blue suit that looked to be a size or two too small for him. His receding brown hair did nothing to distract from his chubby face.

'Hello, madam. My name is Inspector Savage. Judging by your face, along with the fact that everyone else looked in your direction, I'm guessing the knife is familiar to you?'

'It's from my stall.' She pointed towards the three similar knives behind her. 'But I don't know how it ended up in Barry. I was at the food truck.'

'Can I take your details, please?'

Lyndsey gave him her name, then started to relate her

old address before stopping short and rectifying the error.

'So you're not quite sure where you live?'

'Yes, I'm certain. I only moved a couple of days ago, which is why I said my old one, like a reflex.'

'I see,' he said, scribbling in his notepad. 'So what was your relationship with the deceased, Ms Marshall.'

'None, any more. He was my ex. We split up last week.'

'I see,' said the inspector once again.

'And what time did, Barry was it?'

'Yes, Barry Williams.'

'Thank you. What time did Barry Williams meet his end, Ms Marshall?'

Lyndsey paused for a moment. 'I don't know the exact time, why?'

'Well, you are adamant you were at the food truck. You would need the time of death to be certain, would you not?'

Lyndsey became aware of the silence encompassing her but couldn't be sure if everybody had stopped talking to eavesdrop on her conversation or whether her nerves had just blanked everything out. Blood rushed through her ears with the rhythmic thumping of a distant kettle drum.

'No, when I went to the truck he was alive and arguing with someone who I assumed to be a customer. By the time I got back he had disappeared and there was no sign of him again until the wardrobe was opened. So he must have been killed between the time I went for breakfast and when I got back.'

'I see,' said the Inspector again, the words beginning to grate on Lyndsey's consciousness. 'So how long would you say you were gone, Ms Marshall?'

'I'm not sure. Ten, fifteen minutes. I didn't rush, and there was a queue.'

'Can anyone verify your whereabouts during that period?'

'We can,' said Bob. 'I gave her the money to buy us all breakfast. As Lyndsey says, Barry was alive when she left and nowhere to be seen when she got back.'

'Madge at the food truck will remember me.'

'I'm sure she will, Ms Marshall, but without any definitive times who's to say you didn't use a couple of minutes to take revenge on your ex?'

'But ... I didn't. What would be the point? I moved out, moved on. Killing him would make no sense?'

'In my experience, Ms Marshall, things often don't make much logical sense when murder is involved. Would you accompany me to the police station? I'd like to take an official statement from you while the events are fresh in your mind.'

'No, I can't. I have to run the stall. I can come by afterwards, though.'

He paused for a moment. 'OK, I can live with that. Would three o'clock be convenient?'

'The market closes about two, so three would be fine.'

'I look forward to seeing you, Ms Marshall. Try not to be late, if you can help it.'

'I won't,' said Lyndsey, thinking to herself that this day was getting better and better by the minute.

'I'll ask a tech to come across to take your fingerprints and a DNA swab so we can eliminate you as a suspect once the body and murder weapon have been analysed.'

Inspector Savage turned to Bob and Jools and told them an officer would be along to ask them a few questions in a couple of minutes, before ambling back towards the CSI tent.

Lyndsey watched him go. Her stomach was knotted up inside and her mouth was dry.

'Don't you mind him, love,' said Bob putting a hand on her shoulder. 'You didn't do it and he can't twist the facts to put you in the frame. Do you want us to come with you for a bit of support?'

'No, don't be silly. I'll phone a mate.'

'As long as you're sure. Hello, it looks like our turn to be grilled, Jools.' Bob nodded towards a policeman who was making his way across to them. 'If you need anything, Lynds, just say the word.'

'Thanks, I will.'

She walked through the mirrors and waited for the technician. Once he had been, she sat as the police worked their way around everyone. About eleven-thirty they were content and removed the tape to allow the public access to all the stalls other than Barry's and the furniture stall at the end.

The next two hours flew by, busier than she had ever known it. Not that anyone bought anything, but hundreds of people wanted to browse and catch a glimpse of the murder scene. A few asked questions about what had happened, but most appeared as knowledgeable as she was, if not more so. The crowds began to thin out around half past one, so she decided to break the stall down a little early and make her way back.

After putting everything into the van, Lyndsey said 'goodbye' to Bob and Jools, then eased the van out of the pitch and between the remaining market customers towards the exit.

So many thoughts crossed her mind regarding the events of the morning that she all but drove home on autopilot, surprising herself when she arrived. She opened the garage and backed in before carrying the cash box and the photos in through the kitchen door. She placed the float on the table and went up to her room with the photographs.

She took her phone out of her pocket and sat on the edge of the bed, flicking through her contacts. She tried a friend from the newspaper, but the call went straight to voicemail and she disconnected without leaving a message. The next person she rang was visiting Scotland for the weekend.

Lyndsey flicked up and down her contact list, which she now realised was somewhat bereft of car owning friends living near Brentford. She stopped scrolling as a name caught her eye.

Mads. There was a time when she would have been the first name Lyndsey tried, but now it seemed an imposition. How long had it been? It must be two or three years, but they were both to blame for that. Her thumb hovered. Should she? Could she call Mads after all this time to ask a favour?

Mads popped a grape into her mouth absent-mindedly as she stared at the huge television mounted on the wall.

'Come on, Jessica, what are you playing at?' she said to the screen. 'Your friend's trussed up in a van while you're talking to a detective who's paying no attention to you. If I were tied up in a van I'd expect you to be more proactive, girl!'

Not that there was any real doubt in her mind how things would end. Jessica Fletcher had managed to solve the case every time Mads had seen this particular episode, and DVDs weren't best known for changing the outcome of a story between viewings.

A quarter of an hour later, order had been restored and Mads turned off the television before glancing up at the clock.

Half past one. What to do with myself?

She pondered her options, most of which involved visiting one of Chiswick's myriad cafés for a leisurely lunch before heading off to the gym for a couple of hours. Or maybe, a stroll around Gunnersbury Triangle, then onwards for a late lunch. Would it still be lunch then? At what time did lunch morph into tea or dinner? Someone needed to make that decision. The world was a poorer place without important information like that at its fingertips.

Or ... call out for a pizza and watch videos.

Mads shook her head and stood up. It was no good, she had to stop being lazy. Winter would soon be here with all its inducements for slobbing about, and if she let it slide this early she wouldn't like what she saw in the mirror next spring. It wasn't that she was worried about getting huge. Her metabolism had always been on her side there. She just hated the idea of being forced to buy new clothes. It was a control thing. She liked buying new things because she wanted them, not because she had to.

She glanced out of the window and checked the outside temperature before going upstairs to select a light coat and a pair of boots.

Just as she was about to leave the house, her phone rang. She looked at it, expecting a cold call or her husband. To her surprise, the name displayed was Lyndsey.

Lyndsey prodded the screen before she had a chance to change her mind again. Chances are, she would be busy and it would go to voicemail. It was answered after two rings.

'Lynds, I've not heard from you in ages. How are you? We must meet and catch up. Are you still in Hounslow?'

'Hi, Mads. No, I'm back at Grandad's in Brentford. Long story, I'll tell you the whole thing later over a few beers if you're free, but for the moment I need a favour.'

'Of course, hon. What can I do for you? And a drink sounds ideal. Nigel's away on business, as usual, so I'll only be bored in front of the telly.'

Lyndsey paused. 'I realise I'm being cheeky calling you out of the blue like this, but can you give me a ride to Hounslow police station? It shouldn't take long. They want to take a statement and I don't want to worry Grandad by driving the van. He'll know something's up if I do. Is that all right?'

'You're kidding? What happened? You're OK, I hope.'

'Yes, I'm fine. I just need a lift. Are you free now?'

'I'm on my way. Depending on the traffic I should be there in ten or so.'

'Thanks, Mads. I really appreciate it.'

Lyndsey dropped the phone onto the bed and went downstairs again to make some toast. While she was waiting for it to cook, she took the cash box through to the front room.

'Hi, Grandad. Here's the float, but I left the ledger in the van as no one bought anything.'

'Never mind, tomorrow might be busier. Brentford are away today, so anyone interested in programmes was likely at the game. Aside from that, how was your day? I bet you enjoyed seeing everyone from the market again.'

'Yes, I'd forgotten how long it had been. Bob and Jools send their love.'

'I know they were pleased to see you. They must have talked your ears off!'

'You can say that again. I'm grabbing a couple of slices of toast, if you want some, then Mads is coming round and we'll head off for a coffee and a few beers later. Do you want anything before I go?'

'No thanks, I ate lunch earlier. You go and enjoy yourself. Not too much, though. Don't forget you're working again in the morning.'

He winked at her and she leant over to give him a kiss on the cheek before going to the kitchen and slavering some vegan spread on the toast that had just popped up. She went back upstairs and nestled on the bed to eat.

As she chewed, the box of photographs caught her eye so she opened it and started flicking through. None of them showed any famous landmarks allowing her to gauge where they were taken, but she was sure it wasn't England. Her parents were eating outside a café in the first few. They were older than she remembered. She shrugged and figured it must be a quirk of memory, where she had them immortalised in her mind from when she was younger. She carried on through and now they were walking along a street together. Nothing yet indicated where the pictures had been taken. The weather was sunny and warm, wherever they were.

She popped the last of the toast into her mouth just as the doorbell rang. She replaced the lid and put the box into the drawer of her bedside table.

'I'll get it,' she yelled as she hurtled down the stairs. As soon as she opened the door, Mads burst in and gave her a hug.

'Lynds, great to see you. How are you?' she said in her mild, Irish brogue.

Lyndsey waited to be released from the death grip before replying.

'I'm fine, all things considered. You look amazing. You haven't changed one bit.'

Not a single blonde hair was out of place as it cascaded over the shoulders of Mads' black coat. The coat itself looked brand new and expensive. It was open at the front to reveal a smart orange jumper and white blouse, above some immaculate designer jeans. Finishing off her outfit was a pair of boots that probably cost more than Lyndsey's entire wardrobe.

'Wait here, I'll grab a jacket and we can go straight out again.'

Lyndsey filled Mads in on the day's events as they drove to Hounslow.

'That's screwed up. They think you killed him?'

'I'm not sure they do, but I'm a definite suspect until proved otherwise. The inspector isn't giving me much in the way of hope earlier.'

'Ooh, let me guess. He's six foot three, with a barrel chest and dreamy blue eyes?'

'Haha, I'm guessing you're still reading those American cosy mysteries? This is the real world, Mads. Inspector Savage is about five foot eight with a barrel belly and piggy eyes that I didn't catch the colour of.'

'Aww, shame. But what makes him think you would kill someone?'

'The knife came from my stall; I'm fresh out of a relationship with Barry; everyone else at the market appears to be motiveless .... Put like that, even I start to wonder how I did it.'

'Oh don't be daft. You won't even eat animals. I can't imagine you killing Barry, however much he might deserve some severe hurt.'

'I wish you were the Inspector. With any luck, once I give them a statement and they find my prints and DNA don't match anything on the body, that will be the end of the matter.'

'Yes, don't you worry. Everything will turn out fine.'

Mads manoeuvred her way around the back streets and parked in a supermarket car park. They walked the short distance to the police station where they waited behind a small queue of ne'er-do-wells who all appeared to want to report their phones stolen. When they reached the counter, Lyndsey introduced herself to the bored looking policeman behind the glass barrier. He prodded some buttons on the phone in front of him and announced she was here.

'Wait over there, someone will be out for you in a moment,' he said, pointing to the back wall and replacing the handset. Five minutes later a reinforced door opened and Inspector Savage appeared.

'Ms Marshall, this way please.'

He held the door open and Lyndsey and Mads both headed towards him.

'Sorry, Madam,' he said blocking Mads with his arm. 'Unless you're a lawyer, you can wait here.'

'I could be a lawyer.'

'But you're not, are you? Don't worry, she won't be long.' He ushered Lyndsey through the door and let it slam behind them. They walked through an office and into a small interview room.

'Take a seat, Ms Marshall. I need a statement from you listing everything that happened this morning up until the time Barry fell out of the wardrobe. Try to include as many details as possible, things you might think are irrelevant could turn out to be vital.'

He slid a sheet and a pen across the table to her and she started writing. After fifteen minutes, she passed them back.

'That's all, I can't remember anything else.'

Savage read her statement through, referring to his notebook every so often.

'OK, that seems to match the other statements, near enough. No glaring discrepancies, at least. That should be enough for us to be getting along with. One final thing, those are the same clothes you wore earlier, aren't they?'

'Yes, why?' asked Lyndsey.

'We'll need them for testing. I can lend you some overalls to wear if you like, or we can ask your friend to collect something for you from home if you prefer.'

She thought it over and decided not to risk worrying grandad.

'OK, I'll take them, but you're wasting your time. You should be trying to find the guy Barry was arguing with.'

'Yes, Ms Marshall.' Inspector Savage scanned her statement and placed his finger underneath the part he was looking for. 'We will, of course, be rounding up all the largish, stocky men with dark hair in the area and subjecting them to a thorough interrogation. After all, a description as finely honed as that could only fit, oh what would you say? A few thousand?'

'It's not my fault I didn't get a clearer view of him. The sun hadn't risen yet and he had his back to me. I'm sure I'll recognise his gait if I see him again, though. Did no one else manage a better description?'

'You would think, wouldn't you? Nobody was paying much attention, or so they say. Let me find some overalls for you then you can go. For now.'

'What do you mean, "For now."? You can't believe I had anything to do with this?'

'As yet, I don't believe anything. I'm just following the evidence and seeing where it leads. There is a partial fingerprint on the murder weapon and it appears to be yours, so I can't eliminate you as a suspect.'

'But the knife was from my stall. I'm surprised you only found one. Should I make a point of wearing gloves when setting up in future?'

'That depends, Lyndsey. Are you planning on killing somebody else?'

'I didn't kill anyone!'

'So you say, but you must admit it is a little suspicious that Barry disappeared during the same ten minutes you're unaccounted for. Yes, you were seen at the food trailer, but no one can give me definite times. You could have killed him and still bought breakfast given the leeway allowed amongst the statements.

'In fact, while I mention vagueness, you are the only person who has any knowledge of Candy. Aside from family and business associates, the only woman we found on Barry's phone is you. What if Candy doesn't exist at all? Maybe Barry kicked you out after an argument so, intent on revenge, you invented her to muddy the waters a bit.'

Lyndsey stared across the table open-mouthed.

'I don't believe this. How do you think I managed it? I'm five foot three and pretty much all skin and bone. I couldn't lift Barry if I tried all day. Do you think I got his help? How does that play out? "Barry, quick! I've found

Narnia in the back of this wardrobe." And after managing that, I not only used a knife that could be traced straight back to me but left it at the scene. Also, I'm not what you might call an expert, but doesn't stabbing someone generate a lot of blood? My clothing doesn't have a spot on it.'

Savage picked up the sheaf of paper in front of him and jogged it against the desk before placing it back and closing the file.

'All fair points, but forensics will establish whether anything suspicious is on your clothes, and you admit Barry was goading you this morning. Perhaps, in your rage, you saw him slip behind the stalls, grabbed the knife, followed and killed him. Then you hid the body before dashing off to the food van to provide yourself with an alibi. As to the rest, there could be an accomplice to help with the donkey work. Maybe this vague, hefty man who you say was arguing with the victim is better known to you than you're letting on.'

Lyndsey opened her mouth to protest again but decided against it. She bowed her head and glared at the table until Inspector Savage rose to his feet.

'However,' he continued. 'It's all conjecture for the moment. Unless you can think of anything more to add to your statement, I'll arrange a pair of overalls for you and once you change out of those clothes, you can go.'

He left the room and Lyndsey rested her head in her hands. This couldn't be happening. Nothing made sense. How could anybody think she would kill anyone? Why was he even wasting his time concocting ridiculous theories when he should be spending his time finding the real killer? She rubbed her temples and closed her eyes for a few moments until the door reopened and a policewoman entered with some overalls in one hand and a plastic bag in the other.

9

The policewoman guided Lyndsey back through the office and opened the door to let her out to the waiting room. As the door slammed behind her, Mads laughed.

'Oh Janey Mac! Were they out of orange? You should ask them to check again, slate grey isn't your colour.'

'Yeah, yeah. I think you're mixing up real life with American crime drama again. Now take me home and let me change out of this shapeless potato sack before I embarrass you and insist on wearing it to the pub.'

Mads laughed again. 'Oh please do. You wear that all night I'll treat you to dinner as well.' She took her phone from her pocket and waved it in the air. 'Hey, I could ask some of the old gang from Uni to join us.'

Lyndsey glared at her and made for the exit door, hearing Mads chuckling as she followed. She allowed the door to slam shut in faux anger as she left the building and stomped down the walkway.

'Hang on, Lynds.'

Lyndsey stopped and turned to face her. 'What?'

The flash from the phone almost blinded her as Mads started laughing again and caught her up in seconds.

'Come on, Misery-Guts. You'll laugh about this in a few weeks.' She gave her a quick hug. 'Now let's get you back and find something a little more becoming to show off your bony arse to any prospective hotties out on the town tonight.'

'Ugh, I'm sworn off men. Getting drunk will do me fine.'

'Then that's what we shall do, but you'll need to eat first. What says you change then I dump the car at my house and we walk to The Navigator? Just like old times ... well, aside from The Navigator itself, but I haven't been there either since it was refurbished so an adventure for both of us. Sound good?'

Lyndsey smiled. 'OK, you win, but I don't have much money. Somewhere cheaper might be better.'

'Don't worry about that. This is one of the many reasons Nigel keeps my credit cards paid up, and I'm sure he'll love to salve his guilt for being away on business yet another weekend by paying for our night out. So don't argue, you're coming. In fact, while we're here let's buy you something new. After all, you wouldn't want your grandad to catch you sneaking in wearing your prison grey, would you?'

'Oh don't be silly, I couldn't.'

'You can and you will. Come on, shops, food and beer.'

Lyndsey smiled and let Mads drag her towards the shopping mall. There was no point in arguing, it would be awkward if Grandad caught her dressed in a shapeless grey sack. She resolved to pay her back when she found another job.

An hour later Lyndsey was dressed in black jeans, a red t-shirt and a zipped black sweatshirt, along with a gorgeous imitation-leather jacket Mads insisted completed the outfit. She handed the overalls back to the duty officer at the police station and they walked back to the car.

The traffic was kind to them as they drove back through Brentford and twenty minutes later they parked in a private driveway in Chiswick.

Lyndsey stared through the windscreen open mouthed. She knew Mads' in-laws and husband weren't short of a few bob, but she hadn't expected anything quite as elaborate. Ivy covered the front face of the three storey house making it look older than she imagined it was.

'Do you want a tour or shall I drop everything inside and come straight back out?'

'No, no. Always time for a quick nose.'

'Come on.'

Mads got out and opened the back door to collect her bags. By the time Lyndsey had closed her door, Mads was disappearing up the garden path towards the house. The car bipped as she auto-locked the doors, making Lyndsey jump as she broke into a trot to catch her up.

She slammed the front door behind her and followed Mads through a doorway to the left that led to an expansive sitting room. The walls were painted ivory, complementing both the cream carpet and three piece suite. They faced a bronze fire, set into a white fireplace with a round mirror hung on the wall above.

A small alcove to the right was home to an impressive looking grandfather clock, whilst a huge flat-screen television filled the corner to the left. Mads pulled the curtains across the two arched windows facing the front garden and the road. The room was lit by a chandelier far brighter than its delicate appearance suggested it should be.

'This is the lounge, and if you follow me through here ...'. She wandered to the back of the room and through another doorway. Lyndsey followed her down a small flight of stairs. '... to the lower ground floor there's the dining room, kitchen and conservatory.'

An oak table with six chairs sat in the centre of the dining room. They walked across red tiles, past the table and around a pillar into the kitchen.

'Wow, your kitchen and dining room are larger than the flat I shared with Barry. Do you live in the entire house or is it split into flats?'

'The whole thing. Come through here.' Mads flicked a light switch and opened the door to a conservatory. A three seat sofa with a coffee table in front of it rested against the short wall to their left. To the right, a love seat sat next to more steps that Lyndsey assumed led to the hallway on the upper ground floor where they had entered. The roof and the back wall were made of glass.

'This must be lovely in spring and autumn,' said Lyndsey. 'And your garden! It's huge.' She stared out at the lush, green grass floodlit by the security lights Mads had switched on.

'There's a better view of outside from upstairs,' said Mads, climbing the staircase and sliding open a glass door leading to the hallway, as Lyndsey had thought.

Lyndsey followed Mads around the first and second floors before staring through the back window of the converted attic.

'This is stunning, Mads. The garden must be beautiful in the summer. I could only dream of living in a house like this. You're so lucky.'

'I guess.' Mads set off towards the stairs and Lyndsey

followed, switching lights off on each floor as they walked down.

'Your mortgage must be terrifying. Aren't you worried Nigel might lose his job or something?'

'We own it outright. Nigel's father picked it up "cheap" due to an insolvency and handed us the deeds when we got back from honeymoon as a wedding present.'

'You're kidding me?'

'No, though what he considers cheap differs wildly from what you or I might. They have more money scattered about than we could spend in numerous lifetimes.'

'So, do you get on with them?'

'To a point. They seem nice enough, but I always feel as if they are looking down on me. Enough about the in-laws. Let's get ourselves down the pub and start solving your problems.'

They walked in silence through the leafy roads until they reached the river and followed the towpath past the Cow's Tail and beneath the railway bridge. A couple of smokers were standing outside The Navigator, but the breeze from the water was a bit nippy for anyone else to brave the elements. They made their way up the stairs and through the door into an expansive, busy bar.

'This isn't The Navigator I remember,' said Lyndsey. 'How drunk were we?'

'You're not kidding,' agreed Mads as she headed towards the ale pumps. 'Decent choice of beer though. What do you want?'

Lyndsey cast her eyes across the selection.

'Pint of Speckled Hen, please. I'll go hunt us down a table.'

She left Mads trying to catch the serving staff's attention and found a small, round table by the open door to the smoking area out the back. As she sat down, a waitress glided over and asked if she would like a menu.

'Two, please.' She took the offered menus and the waitress disappeared again. 'Mind you, we'll need to find a bigger table first,' she muttered to herself as she put them down, covering most of it.

She picked one up and glanced through. Everything marked with a *V* contained cheese or egg. She placed the menu back onto the table and sat back in her chair to peruse the bar.

The conversation in the pub appeared convivial at first, but on closer examination the volume was a few notches louder than necessary to be heard above the background music. Her attention was drawn to the corner where a man kept bursting into loud guffaws. Judging by the ages of the young women he was trying to impress, he still thought he had a full head of hair and twenty or thirty fewer years.

She decided to be charitable and imagine he was an art or writing tutor chilling with his students after a day's lessons. Most of the other customers were couples who were spread amongst the nearby tables or groups of men herding at the bar.

To her right, though, sat on a sofa and armchairs around a spacious coffee table were the loudest group of women she had ever encountered. They must have started early. One had a voice so piercing, Lyndsey expected the glass in the back windows to shatter at any moment. Every time she spoke, the others all cackled in laughter, like hyenas with a fresh carcass.

She watched as Mads made her way across the pub

carrying the beer. Her blonde hair flowed across her shoulders as she walked, appearing oblivious to the appreciative stares she was getting from the groups of men as she passed. Lyndsey knew better though, and could see Mads was well aware of the number of eyes tracking her progress. She placed a couple of pints on the table as she sat down.

'Here you go. What's up, your face is a picture?'

'What's happened to our pub? Where is the cosy little bar we used to hang out in? The old Navigator wouldn't have attracted Foghorn Bill, behind you, or the haw–haw-whores over there.' She tipped her head in the direction of the cackling horde. 'Don't tell me we were like that ten years ago.'

'Not that I recall,' said Mads, her mischievous smile flitting across her lips, 'but then again, will they remember tonight in years to come?'

'Stop it, and don't give me that look. After the week I've had I deserve to get grumpy without your dinky little smile cajoling me out of it.'

'Like my old Grandma used to say, "Smile regardless of how you feel. It exasperates everyone who was trying to annoy you in the first place."'

Lyndsey picked up her pint and took a long, slow drink to hide the grin that was threatening to burst out at any moment.

'I can't believe how long it's been since we last hung out. Didn't we make a pinky promise that we would never let relationships get in the way of our friendship?'

Mads sighed. 'I know, but it turns out we are like "those girls" after all. On behalf of eighteen year old Mads, may I say that I'm disappointed in the pair of us.'

She theatrically raised her glass and took a mouthful of beer. 'Me in particular. You had the excuse of a job that took up most of your waking hours, but I came back from my honeymoon and retreated behind the walls of my ivory tower. Sorry, I kept meaning to suggest going somewhere, I just never got around to it.'

'Hey, we're both to blame. After four years at uni and another three living in each others' pockets trying to drink Brentford dry and binge-watch every film and classic series going, I'm sure we needed a bit of a break. The longer it went on though, the more difficult it became to get back together again.'

Mads glanced at the menus. 'Did you find anything to eat?'

'No, nothing vegan apart from maybe mix and matching a few sides. Let's drink this first then worry about food afterwards. We'll need a better table as well, unless they've gone all nouveau and are going to serve us on saucers.'

'Ha, that might even wipe the smile off my face. So, aside from the past week, what have you been up to?'

Lyndsey sighed. 'The last three years have flown by. I had a job with the local paper covering church fêtes and school sports days, until they figured they didn't need any more of that in-depth, hard-hitting journalism from me.'

'What about your other writing?'

'I've been too busy. Cats don't rescue themselves from trees, and if a cat gets rescued from a tree without a local reporter to report it, did the cat get rescued at all?'

'Oh, stop feeling so sorry for yourself. You com-plain about me reading trashy books, but until you write something better to occupy my time I'm not going t[...] be changing my habits. You've seen what I do every d[...] I sit around my beautiful house, bored out of my mi[...] Trust me, watching cats get rescued from trees woul[...] a highlight. Of course, I live in Chiswick where al[...] a have double-barrelled names and aren't allowed [...] the house in case they get frisky with a stray tabl[...] Brentford, so no tree climbing for them.'

Lyndsey laughed. 'Maybe I can find a part[...] and write novels in my spare time. But you [...] done something? Don't you visit your famil[...] to time?'

'Lynds, Wexford is a beautiful county, b[...]

61

dreds of relatives and while I love them to bits, all they do since the wedding is gather round to ask what's wrong with me. They can't understand the concept of being married three years without having at least a couple of kids and another on the way. They are well-meaning, but hard work. I encourage my parents and sisters to visit as often as possible. I pay for their flights, put them up at the house and show them all the tourist spots they want to see and a few more for good measure, but they have lives of their own. The only person who no longer has one is me.'

Mads paused for a moment and took a long drink of her beer. 'But all that's changed now. I have a friend in trouble and all the time in the world to help solve the mystery of her dead rat of an ex-boyfriend.'

Lyndsey flinched as the haw-haw-whores launched into another burst of raucous cackling to her right.

'Well, if we're going to eat let's find another table.'

As she stood to get a better view of the pub, a man came in from the smoking area behind them. As he walked past and headed towards the river door, she froze.

'He's the guy who was arguing with Barry, I'd swear to it. Quick, drink up. We can follow him.'

'Why?' asked Mads, draining her glass in one fluid motion.

'If we find out where he lives, we can ...'

'Can what?'

'I don't know, but unless we move now we'll lose him. Come on.'

Lyndsey finished her pint and set off with Mads in hot pursuit. As they reached the towpath they saw the man walking beneath a tree in the direction of Kew Bridge and scurried off after him.

'Are you sure it's him?' asked Mads.

'Yes, I'm certain from the way he walks. The rolling sailor's gait but favouring his right leg as if he's got an injury on his left side. That's the way he walked across to Barry's stall when he first arrived this morning. I told the police I'd recognise him from his walk, but struggled to describe it without seeing it again. It has to be him.'

'OK, but he's huge. We find where he's going then call someone. I'm not confronting him.'

'Sounds like a plan. Let's make sure we don't lose him.'

A couple in a motorboat tuk-tukked past them on the almost full river, making the water lap the bank. On some days, high tide would cover the walkway, but they were lucky tonight. A squirrel darted into the middle of the path and stared at them, as if challenging their right of way, but raced up a tree to observe them from the branches as they scurried past.

They passed the Gong & Cap and followed the man across Kew Bridge. He turned his head a couple of times to glance at the river but they were too far behind to discern any facial details even with the bright street lights overhead.

A gust of wind blew across the bridge and Lyndsey smiled at the multi-coloured patterns dancing across the ripples on the water.

The Thames is pretty after dark. I wish we had more time to appreciate it.

They continued along the road until the man followed a pathway across Kew Green. As they also started to cross the Green, he disappeared through the front door of the Fiacre and Unicorns, or the FU as many locals referred to the sizeable hotel pub.

'Hope he's going for a drink. We'll never find him if he's staying in the hotel itself,' said Lyndsey.

'Ooh, but think of the added excitement. What if he's an international assassin, hired by some shady Mr Big?'

'Ha, yeah right. To kill Barry? The only way that

works is if he was so inept he got the wrong person.'

Lyndsey opened the door and led Mads into the entrance hall. She turned right into the bar and was pleased to find the man sitting on a barstool watching rugby on the television in the corner, along with twenty or thirty other guys scattered around.

'Grab that table,' said Mads indicating to their right. 'I'll get the beers and some menus.'

Lyndsey sat down in an armchair that had looked far more comfortable than it was. No matter, at least she had a clear view of their suspect. Mads soon joined her and put two pints on the table.

'I checked for vegan stuff with the barman and he assured me the giant cous cous was fine, so I ordered two. Is that OK, or shall I see if I can change it?'

'No, that sounds lovely. Thanks. What was the beer selection like?'

'Same as ever. I got a couple of Specials, we had many a good night on this little darling.'

Lyndsey picked up her drink and took a long sip. 'Slides down every bit as smoothly as I remember. We must make a point of coming here more often.'

'So what's our killer up to?'

Lyndsey glanced over Mads' shoulder.

'He's content watching the rugby. I hope he stays to

the end of the game, that will give us time to eat. It might look suspicious if we go charging off partway through a meal.'

'I think we should be safe. I've never come across a man walk into a pub to watch sport and leave before it finishes. I think it's genetic.'

Ten minutes later, the barman brought over their food. Lyndsey breathed in the aroma and realising how hungry she was, set about devouring it without delay causing Mads to laugh.

'Geez, girl. There are lions on David Attenborough with more decorum. No one's going to steal it, you know.'

'Easy for you to say. I'm starving, and the last thing I want is to leave any if we need to make a quick exit.'

Mads shook her head and started to eat. A short while later, a loud cheer went up from the rugby crowd and Lyndsey glanced over.

'Oh crap. I think he might be going.'

Their prey stood up and walked away from them towards the toilets. After a while he returned and bought another pint. She let out a sigh of relief.

'False alarm, must be half time. Shall I go and grab us more beer?'

'Don't you bloody dare,' said Mads, spraying cous cous everywhere. 'I told you, tonight's on Nigel. Give me two minutes and I'll get us another round.'

'If you say so, but try to be a little more ladylike with your eating, will you? What would your neighbours say about that performance?' She took a drink to hide the smile on her lips.

'Touché,' said Mads. She drank her beer and went to the bar. When she got back they polished off their meal, listening to the background noise of the rugby fans as they cheered and groaned their way through the second half. Once the match finished, their man downed the rest of his pint.

'OK, I think this might be it,' said Lyndsey, trying to appear casual as she also drained her glass. 'Drink up, here he comes.'

He lumbered by them as Mads drank up and when they heard the front door open, they both started to follow. The wind was chilly after the warmth of the pub and Lyndsey put her hands into her pockets and drew her jacket tight around her as they checked to see where he had gone.

'There he is,' she whispered and turned right along the pavement.

They walked alongside the Green until he turned left at the duck pond and headed for another pub.

Mads sighed. 'Do you think he's on to us and plans

to get us so drunk we're not capable of following him any farther?'

They entered The Whippet and followed him through the bar. As they reached the back door, he turned right at the back of the beer garden.

'Ooh, tricky. Taking a short cut through the pub. Hurry up, we don't want to lose him in the alleyways.'

The thought of alleyways made Lyndsey shudder, but she pushed the memories of hundreds of film noir movies to the back of her mind and picked up the pace a little. He turned left into an alley leading to the river. At the corner they watched his silhouette make its way along a scantily lit path before climbing a flight of stairs at the end and turning right onto the towpath.

They headed after him, past a small terrace of houses with a streetlight outside. Lyndsey studied them as they passed. None had any lights on. They reached a bend in the river and found themselves in a natural tunnel formed by bushes and trees arching over the pathway. The sudden change in visibility rendered them both temporarily blind and Mads grabbed Lyndsey's arm as they edged forwards.

'You sure he didn't go into one of those houses back there?' she whispered.

'I don't think so. None of them had any lights on. I can't believe how dark it is with the light from across the river blocked out by the foliage.'

They walked for a few more metres before Mads stopped, her vice-like grip on Lyndsey's arm forcing her to stop too.

'Wouldn't we hear footsteps if he was ahead of us?'

'I'm not sure. The wind rustling through the trees is enough to obscure most sounds like that. How much further until we get some lighting or a break in the bushes?'

'No idea. I've only walked along here in the daytime. This tunnel is lovely when the sun shines through the leaves, but it's fast losing its charm. Let's go back.'

Lyndsey thought for a moment. 'Not yet. We've come all this way. Let's keep going a bit longer. There's sure to be a light somewhere.'

Mads sighed, but started edging forwards again. After a minute or so she stopped again.

'Come on, this is crazy. Even if he did come this way, he must be so far ahead of us by now we'll never catch him.'

Lyndsey's shoulders sagged in defeat as she realised Mads was talking sense. 'OK, you win. It is spooky. You don't realise how much we take streetlights for granted until you do something like this.'

They turned round and walked three or four steps before being stopped in their tracks by a blinding light. A gruff voice broke the silence.

'Good evening, ladies. Why are you following me?'

Mads turned and fled. In her panic, hurtling into darkness seemed the most natural thing in the world. Despite stumbling a couple of times, she kept her feet and ran for a minute or two before stopping and leaning against a tree trunk to catch her breath.

The light still glowed bright in her eyes, obscuring her vision, not that she imagined there was much to see. She tried to listen, but the blood rushing through her ears obscured any other sounds. Where was Lyndsey? She had expected her to be right behind her.

The guy must have seen them following and hidden to let them pass before enacting an ambush.

How could I allow that to happen? Haven't I watched and read enough murder mysteries to be able to predict that exact scenario?

She pulled her phone out of her pocket and blinked a

few times until her eyes focused on the screen. Damn, no signal. She put it back and weighed her options.

Returning the way she had come didn't appeal. Better to continue along the towpath as far as the railway bridge, then she could call Lyndsey, and if necessary, the police. She set off, steadily this time, making sure she kept to the right hand side of the path away from the water. Tripping over and falling through the bushes into the river wouldn't improve matters.

Her eyes were playing tricks on her. She could see hundreds of tiny pinpricks, like fly vision was always depicted in film. The effect was unsettling and she picked up her pace a little.

Out of nowhere, a red flashing light appeared at about knee height, heading for her at a fair rate of knots. She stopped and let out a startled squeal. A bicycle skidded to a halt and in the gloom she struggled to make out three characters. A cyclist, a jogger and a dog; the dog being the only one of the three with the sense to be illuminated.

'Sorry,' said the man on the bike.

The jogger grabbed the dog's collar and guided it closer to her, then they continued on their way, disappearing into the darkness.

Mads could feel her heart beating so hard it seemed fit to burst. She took a few deep breaths to settle herself then took a couple more steps before stopping again.

'Geez, you're a daft cow, Madeleine,' she muttered. She took the phone from her pocket again and selected the notes app so she could use the bright, white background as a makeshift torch.

Note to self. Find a flashlight app when you get home.

While not perfect, the light enabled her to walk at a decent pace and before long she rounded a corner and the railway bridge appeared ahead of her. Her phone pinged, announcing a new message had arrived.

'Oh, now you manage a signal. Well, you can wait until I'm standing safely in the glow of the lights.'

A wave of relief rolled over her as she reached the streetlights, and she quit the app to check her messages.

One missed call, one new text.

Both from Lyndsey.

14

Lyndsey closed her eyes against the dazzling light and felt a tug on her arm as Mads peeled away and scampered off. She half turned to follow, but the man grabbed her.

'Let me go!', she said as she struggled against his grip.

'So you'd rather run off after your mate into total darkness than say why you're following me? I don't know who you think I am, but I'm sure I'm not that guy.'

Lyndsey paused and took some deep breaths. 'You were at the market earlier.'

'Yes. And?'

She blinked a few times to try to make her vision return to normal. 'I'm not comfortable talking to you here. Let's go back to the pub. I'll feel safer with people about.'

He thought for a moment. 'OK, fair enough. What about your friend?'

Lyndsey turned to face away from him and yelled.

'Mads!'

The only response was silence.

'I'll call her. The speed she took off at, she could be in Hammersmith by now. Come on, let's walk back to the lights.'

It only took a minute or so for them to reach the houses again with the aid of the torch. Lyndsey took out her phone and rang, but it went straight to voicemail. She hung up and texted instead. Neither of them spoke until they were nearing The Whippet.

'I'm John, by the way. What do you reckon? Pint in here or back to the FU?'

'Think I'd rather the FU, and it'll be easier for Mads, assuming she makes her way back along the road. And I'm Lyndsey.'

'OK Lyndsey. The FU it is. After you.'

He indicated towards the back garden of The Whippet with its year-round fairy lights presenting an other-worldly ambience when approached from this direction.

'We're going to cut through? Bit cheeky, isn't it?'

'We did the other way. If you feel guilty, just act as if you're looking for someone.'

Lyndsey dug her hands into her jacket pockets and made her way through the pub feeling as if everyone's eyes were on her. As she reached the front and opened the door to leave, the barman shouted, 'Goodnight'.

'Night,' replied John as he followed her out.

As they passed the duck pond Lyndsey's phone rang and she pulled it from her pocket and glanced at the screen before answering.

'Mads. Are you OK?'

'A bit shaken, but no major injuries. How about you?'

'Yes, fine. We'll be back in the FU in a minute.'

'We?'

'I'm with John, the man we were following.'

The line went quiet for a few seconds.

'I thought you said he was the killer.'

'Yeah, we might need to rethink that. I figured it was better to talk to him in a pub full of people rather than alone in the dark. Does that make sense?'

'So you're saying I ran my heart out, terrified, along a towpath where I had to contend with trees, roots, bushes, dogs, bikes and joggers, all so we can do what we could have done twenty minutes ago when we were all three in the pub the first time round?'

'Well, when you put it like that ... we're here now. See you in a few.' Lyndsey hung up.

'She's still alive then?' asked John as they walked up to the bar. 'What can I get you both?'

'Yes, though she isn't as pleased as she might that I

haven't been abducted and locked in a cellar. We'll have pints of Special, please.'

He looked around. 'The round table by the fire's emptying out if you want to go grab it.'

Lyndsey made her way past the few remaining rugby fans who had been watching the game earlier. She sat at the far side of the table and warmed her hands by the fire. They were shaking, whether through shock or cold she wasn't sure. John put three pints on the table and parked himself in the chair next to her.

'Right, so why were you following me and why would I abduct you?' he asked before taking a drink. 'Don't get me wrong, I'm sure you'd make a fine decorative addition to any cellar, but my house didn't come fitted with one.'

She took a long sip from her pint and gave John the once over. He seemed ordinary enough, a mop of unkempt brown hair over a squarish face and he wore a hip length leather coat over a red sweatshirt that hugged his not inconsiderable bulk. He had the physique of an ex-rugby player who had put on a few kilos since giving up playing. Lyndsey guessed he must be about 35 or 40.

'You came to the market this morning and argued with Barry.'

'Yes, not long after opening time.'

'Well, I couldn't hear exactly what you were saying

but you were angry with him.'

'Right again, I was bloody furious. He sublets that pitch from my old man. Thing is he's been falling behind on his payments and every time my dad tried to talk to him he fobbed him off with one excuse after another. I figured a visit from me would be more effective. Told him he either settles his debt by the end of the month or finds himself another market stall.'

'That was it? You didn't fight or anything?'

'No, just gave him a piece of my mind and said I'd be back in a couple of weeks for the money. Then I went to work. I open up at 7.30 so couldn't waste much time on him. Why, what did he say to you?'

'Well, nothing. I went to the food stall while you were arguing. By the time I got back he was missing. As I saw you were having a heated row, I wondered if anything had happened.'

'Not while I was around. I shouted at him a bit and stormed off. I made my point. Not that any of this explains why you and Mads were following me?'

'Someone murdered Barry while I was at the food truck and, as an angry stranger, you seemed the most likely person to have done it.'

'Barry's dead? That's an unexpected turn. What was he to you?'

Lyndsey took another long sip. 'I had a messy break-up with him last week. That, coupled with him being killed with a dagger from my stall, means the police have me perched on top of their suspect list.'

'So you and your mate are playing detective?'

'It beats sitting around doing nothing and the local cops aren't as dynamic or smart as the ones on TV.'

John laughed. 'I imagine they're not. How did you find out who I was?'

'Pure luck. We were in The Navigator and you happened to walk through. I recognised your gait from this morning.'

'Ah right, the limp from my old football injury stands out I suppose. Well, it wasn't me, so what are you going to do now?'

Mads entered the bar with a frown on her face and headed in their direction.

'Bear with me a moment,' said Lyndsey, standing and walking across to meet her.

'Where were you? Why didn't you follow me?'

'I'm sorry,' said Lyndsey, giving Mads a hug. 'I tried but John grabbed my arm. By the time I figured he wasn't going to hurt us, you were gone. I yelled as loud as I could, but you must have been too far away to hear.'

She pulled back.

'Then again, where were you? Once you realised you were alone, why didn't you come back and check?'

'I panicked. Your eyes and mind start playing tricks when you run into complete darkness. You have no idea.'

'Well, we're safe and back together again. Come and sit down with John. He got you a pint in.'

'I would hope so, after that scare. He could have killed the both of us.'

'Stop over-dramatising. He's normal enough. Come on.'

They sat at the table.

'So, John. Lyndsey tells me you're not a murderer.'

'Sorry to disappoint you, though it has to be a plus point for her that I'm not.'

She picked up her glass and drank half its contents before putting it back on the table and sighing. 'So if he isn't the killer, what are we going to do now?'

Lyndsey shrugged. 'Get drunk I guess. You can come to the market in the morning and try to get some information from the other stallholders. One of them must have seen something, but they might be more likely to tell you than me or the police.'

'Why would they tell me anything?'

'They don't know who you are, so if you turn up with a notebook and a pen you can pretend to be a reporter.

You'll be surprised what people will say to the press or television cameras that they wouldn't say to anyone else.'

Mads sat up straight and grinned. 'Oh, I like that. Madeleine Walsh, intrepid reporter. Will I need a dirty old mac and a trilby?'

Lyndsey laughed.

'No, we'll hold back on the full 40s experience until our investigations lead us to the Isle of Wight. I sometimes wonder about you, Mads. You must have seen a film based around a newsroom that was made in colour?'

'Yes, but you can't beat the classics. So, John. If you're not a murderer, what do you do?'

'I'm manager at a builders' merchants. Nothing as exciting as the life you two are currently leading, but if you want building materials at trade prices, I'm your man. How about you?'

'Lots of watching DVDs and gym time to counteract its effects. I need to get a hobby. I can feel myself vegetating.'

'Yes, you should,' said Lyndsey. 'What happened to your drawing and painting? I'll tell you, John. She was so talented at University we all expected her to be the most likely to succeed.'

'Oh, come on now. I wasn't that good. How about your creative writing? You've let that slip by the by over the past few years.'

'Don't try to wriggle out of the spotlight. With the size of your house you could make room for a studio. It would be more interesting than watching old shows on TV, wouldn't it?'

'I'll think about it. Do you two want another pint?'

Lyndsey nodded.

'John?'

'No thanks. I'd better get going. Early start in the morning. Nice to meet you both and if you need any help with the case give me a call.' He handed Lyndsey a business card as he stood up. 'But try to avoid the temptation to follow strange men along dark alleys and towpaths in future. They're not all as mild-mannered as I am.'

'I'll make a point of remembering that,' she said as he turned away and headed for the door.

'Hey, both of us playing detective is like the adventure we had at uni, isn't it?' said Mads.

'Goodness, I hope not. That scared the life out of me.'

'Come on, now. A bit of excitement is good for the soul.'

'Says you, the woman who just broke the land speed record along the towpath.'

'I'm out of practice, that's all. I'll soon have my bravery levels recharged.'

'We'll see, though we're back to having no leads again.'

'Don't be so sure. John gave you his card and they reckon the guilty always try to get in on the investigation, don't they?'

Mads went to the bar leaving Lyndsey shaking her head in bemusement.

Lyndsey sat up with a start. She peered through bleary eyes as vague memories of her staggering back from the pub, arm in arm with Mads played through her mind.

What is that racket?

She rubbed her eyes and blinked as they cleared, homing in on her phone that was vibrating its way around the bedside table. She picked it up and stabbed the screen to stop the ringtone waking the entire street.

'Mornin' you dirty stop-out. How are you feeling?'

'Ugh, Grandad.' Lyndsey slumped back and laid on the pillow again. 'What's the time?'

'Five o'clock, love. I was figuring you might still be over the limit, so how about I drive the van round for you? You can head straight to the market rather than coming here first.'

Five o'clock! No one should be up at this time on a Sunday unless they haven't gone to bed yet!

'Yes, please. If you don't mind.'

'OK, I'll leave the keys with Bob.' He laughed. 'So, did you get lucky last night?'

'Grandad, stop it! I walked Mads back and by the time we got here it was late so it made sense to stay.'

'Whatever you say, sweetheart. So I imagine I'll be putting up with you for another week?'

'Yes. There was a queue of multi-millionaires begging me to marry them, but I turned them all down just to spite you. Happy?'

'You know me, love. I'm always happy. Get yourself up and grab something to eat. I'll drive to the market for you. OK?'

'Sounds good. Thanks.'

She hung up and held the phone against her chest while she closed her eyes again. She wanted to doze off for another ten minutes or so, but the urge to pee won out and she threw the quilt off and powered herself vertical. A few seconds later she collapsed back on the bed in a dizzy heap.

Let's try that again, just a little slower.

This time she managed and staggered off to the bathroom. After a quick shower she felt semi-human again and made her way to the stairs, knocking on Mads' door on the way.

'Mads, time to get up. I'll rustle up some breakfast while you get ready.'

A grunt sounded from behind the door and she went downstairs where she found a freezer filled with enough goodies to stock a small health shop. Before long the kitchen smelt of coffee and bacon, or at least as close as vegan rashers get.

Mads bounded around the corner, looking far more alive than Lyndsey felt.

'Wow, that smells fantastic. Keep this up and your grandad will have competition for your services. Do you need a hand with anything?'

'No, you sit down. I'm almost done.'

Mads poured them both coffee and sat at the table.

'I thought we needed to leave by now?'

'Yes, we did, but Grandad's going to drive the van to the market. For some reason he thought I might be too drunk to manage.' She brought over a tray containing bowls of sausages, bacon, baked beans, mushrooms and tomatoes along with a full toast rack and some spread. 'Legally I'm sure he's right and the last thing I need right now is an arrest for drinking and driving.'

'Aww, he's a sweetheart,' said Mads, helping herself to a decent portion of everything on offer. 'I hope you told him to wear a blindfold.'

Lyndsey stared quizzically for a moment before raising a hand to her mouth to obscure a gasp. 'Oh no, after trying to keep the murder a secret from him. Do you think the police will have taken the tape and tent down by now so everything looks normal?'

'Yes, I expect that's exactly what's happened. Not only that, everyone he knows at the market will forget to mention it to him, and at this very moment a gang of elves are setting up your stall to save you the trouble. Because your life is panning out like that at the moment, Lynds.'

Lyndsey put her head in her hands. 'Ah well. Nothing I can do now. I didn't want him worrying about me, that's all.'

'Don't you mind him, he's a tough old dog. So how shall we do this today?'

'If we aim to arrive about six or so, you can drink a cup of coffee in the café over the road while I go in and set up. That way no one will think we know each other. Do you have a notepad?'

Mads got up and trotted off. She came back a couple of minutes later brandishing a pad and pen.

'So do I come to you first, or come from the other side and finish at your stall?'

'Start with Ranjit on the corner and work round.

Once everyone's been questioned, make your way back to me as if you're asking supplementary questions. Here, give me the notepad and I'll write everybody's names down for you.'

'Sounds like a plan,' said Mads, handing it across and tucking into her breakfast as if she hadn't eaten for days.

By the time they reached the café Lyndsey's head had stopped spinning and she bought herself a tea to take away along with a mug of coffee for Mads.

'Here you go. Wait here until 6.30 or so, when the market opens. You know where I am, don't you?'

'Don't worry, I'll find you. You get going and I'll follow you across in half an hour.'

The alcove looked strange with the police tape and large white tent still covering much of Bill and Rhonda's pitch. Barry's stall was bare, but also taped off. She assumed his stock had been removed as evidence.

She strolled up to Bob and Jools.

'Hi, did Grandad leave the van keys with you?'

'Here you go, Lynds,' said Bob, holding them out to her. 'You didn't tell him about the excitement yesterday?'

'I didn't get time. I had to give that statement then went to the pub.'

'How did that go? The police, I mean. I have a fair idea how having a drink goes.'

'Doesn't he just,' said Jools.

'As well as could be expected. I don't like Inspector Savage. He kept implying I had done it.'

'Don't you worry about him,' said Jools. 'We all know you're innocent and he'll never prove otherwise. I like that outfit you're wearing, is it new?'

Lyndsey glanced down at herself. 'Yes, they wanted my clothes for forensics so I picked up a few new bits and returned the shapeless overalls they gave me. I'd best get set up. Catch you in a bit.'

'Chin up, love. Everything will sort itself out,' said Bob as he gave her a quick hug before returning to finish displaying the mirrors.

She started laying everything out, smiling as she listened to Bob and Jools bickering behind the next stall. Some things never changed, she thought.

'I tell you, Martin got lucky last night. He hasn't been home. He was wearing that UK Subs sweatshirt yesterday.'

'No, he had a Ramones shirt on. I remember because I had the exact same logo on a t-shirt until it fell apart through old age.'

'You're wrong, because I thought it was a funny coincidence that he wore the UK Subs C.I.D. design on the day the police were buzzing around. And don't give me that old age nonsense. Your t-shirts self-destruct because you grow too fat for them.'

Lyndsey imagined Bob sucking in his belly.

'Don't start. The washing machine shrinks all my stuff.'

'Maybe you should learn to use it yourself. I'm sure it wouldn't dare do such a thing if you were in charge.'

'Oh, my fault is it?'

'Of course, but you must be used to that by now, sweetie.'

Lyndsey looked around and saw Jools give him a quick peck on the cheek. 'Give up, Bob. You're never going to win.'

'Oh great!' he said, rolling his eyes to the sky. 'Now they're ganging up on me.'

16

Mads watched Lyndsey cross the road and walk through the market gates. She couldn't believe how excited she was to be up at this unearthly hour playing detective. How had she allowed her life to become so dull? Yes, the house was gorgeous and the almost unlimited spending she could do had been exciting at first, but the cost of that was a husband she seldom saw and a mind-boggling selection of television shows that she did.

Why had it taken Lyndsey to be suspected of murder and phone up out of the blue for her to realise? Was she really that shallow?

She promised herself that things were going to change. Being a lady of leisure had been fine for a while, but she had stagnated long enough. Once they caught the murderer, she would give serious thought to her future.

She sipped her coffee and pretended to read a newspaper while trying to listen to the other conversations in the café. Not that there was anything of interest being discussed. Maisie had been taken to hospital with complications, Julia's dog had given birth to a litter of puppies, and the couple sitting at the window table on the other side of the door were planning a trip to Tenerife. Of course, Mads had no idea who Maisie and Julia were, so was happy to cross them off her mental list of suspects. The Tenerife-bound couple were in their late 50s and didn't come across as ruthless criminals fleeing to Spain to evade justice, so she crossed them off too.

Well, she reasoned, if it was going to be that easy, it wouldn't be much of a mystery.

Time ticked by and she was about to drink up and head off when the two girls behind her made her prick her ears up.

'Did you hear about that murder over the market yesterday?'

'Yeah, that record stall bloke, Barry.'

'Do you think Sharon knows?'

'No clue. I wouldn't blame her if she killed him, to be honest.'

'Oh don't. You shouldn't say things like that. She's been through enough.'

Mads studied them in the reflection of the window.

They were young, no older than 20 and judging by their uniforms they worked at the supermarket down the road. She turned around in her chair to speak to them.

'Hey, ladies. I'm a reporter looking into the murder. Could I buy you both a cup of tea and have a quick chat?'

'We don't know nothing,' said the bleached blonde across the table. She had a pale, thin face and clumsily applied eye makeup.

'I'll take that chance. If you tell me something that leads to finding the killer, you might get your pictures in the paper and everything.'

Both girls sat up a little straighter. Mads glanced across at the counter and perused what was on offer behind the glass. 'What says a cup of tea and a slice of chocolate cake each?'

The blonde looked at her mate who shrugged back at her. 'I shouldn't. What do you think, Shirl?'

Mads looked at Shirl. She had a rounder face than her friend, framed by shoulder length brown hair and bangs. She also had over-heavy eye makeup, but it had been applied with a little more care.

'I won't tell if you don't.'

'Oh go on, but we can't sit here long. Our boss will do her nut if we're late.'

Mads got up and went to the counter, returning with

two mugs of tea and two slices of cake.

'Thanks. So what paper do you write for?'

'I'm freelance. Sell my stuff to anyone and everyone.'

'Would we know you?'

'Maybe,' she said, pretending to search through her pockets for a card. 'I'm out of business cards, I keep meaning to order some more. My name's Madeleine.' She thought for a moment. 'Madeleine Monroe.'

'Oh wow,' said Shirl. 'I think I've heard your name somewhere before.'

'That's nice,' said Mads, stifling a laugh. 'So tell me, who is Sharon?'

'Oh no,' said the blonde. 'I didn't mean it when I said she might have killed him. It was a joke.'

'I'm sure she didn't, but if she knew Barry she can give me some background details. The more I can find out about the victim, the easier it will be to find out why he was murdered.'

'As long as I won't be getting her into bother. And isn't it up to the Old Bill to find whoever did it?'

'There's nothing wrong with giving the police a helping hand, and if it means I get an exclusive, so much the better. And you won't get Sharon into trouble, I promise. I want to chat to her, like we're doing now. Who is she and what's her connection to him?'

'I don't suppose it'll do any harm. What do you think, Shirl?'

Shirl shrugged again. 'Up to you, Jacks. We only have her number, so if she doesn't want to talk she can hang up, can't she?'

'I s'pose. Here you go.'

Jacks prodded at her phone a few times and pushed it across to Mads with Sharon's number displayed on the screen. Mads wrote it down.

'She used to work with us but don't know if she still does. She's been off a while.'

'How did she know Barry?'

'She was going out with him. They split up a couple of months back.'

Well, this is going to be news to Lyndsey.

'Why did they break up?'

'She got pregnant. He didn't want anything to do with her after that.'

'Wow, that's not cool.'

'Yeah, right? It was no surprise to us. We knew what he was like, but Sharon didn't. Thought the sun shone out of his ... you know.'

'So where did you both meet him?'

'We only met him the once. We were down the pub and they came in so they joined us at the table.'

'So why didn't you like him?'

'He was a creep. Sharon went for a pee and he started hitting on us. He was shameless, wasn't he Shirl.'

'Shameless, Jacks.'

'Did you tell Sharon?'

'No, didn't like to. He'd have said he was joking around and we misunderstood or something. She wouldn't have believed us. We weren't best mates or anything, only work colleagues.'

Mads scanned her notes.

'You say she hasn't been at work. Where has she been?'

Shirl and Jacks glanced at each other and both took a mouthful of cake. If there was an Olympic category for synchronised cake eating, they would be contenders for the gold on that evidence. Mads waited patiently. She must have touched a nerve. After sloshing the cake down with a gulp of tea, Jacks broke the silence.

'She's been in hospital. When Barry dumped her she tried to kill herself. Swallowed a bunch of pills. Her parents found her just in time and rushed her to A&E.'

'But she's OK now?'

'So we were told. She lost the baby and spent a while in the psych unit but they let her out a couple of weeks back. Like I said, I don't know if she's coming back to work.'

Shirl glanced at the clock above the counter. 'Speaking of which, we'd best be moving. Thanks for the tea and cake.'

'You're welcome. Could I take your full names and numbers, please? Just in case the newspaper needs to contact you for verification or photos before the story goes to print.'

She passed her notepad across so they could fill in their details. Not that she expected to need them, but better safe than sorry. When they had finished she picked it up and stood.

'Lovely to meet you both. Hope you don't get in trouble for being late on my account.'

'We'll be OK,' said Jacks. 'Tell us if we're going to be in the paper won't you.'

'I will,' said Mads turning towards the door. 'Thanks again.'

17

Having laid out her wares, Lyndsey sat on the stool and scanned the alcove. It was quieter than normal, even taking the time of day into account. The lack of music from Barry's stall gave the market an eerie atmosphere, but on top of that the usual banter she was accustomed to was also missing. Those in conversation were huddled closely as if conspiring together in some dastardly plot, and no one wanted to catch her eye. She checked her phone at quarter to seven and looked towards Ranjit, expecting Mads to be talking to him, but there was no sign of her. There was another strange thing. Where had she got to?

A man approached her stall. He had clean-cut mahogany hair, and beneath his overcoat he wore a dark suit with a white shirt and tie. She laughed to herself, thinking Mads would mark him down as some kind of government agent or assassin, though she felt it more likely he might be a police detective or something.

'Hi,' she said as he stopped in front of the stall. He didn't reply, just inspected everything she had laid out.

'Do you have any photos?' he asked.

Lyndsey shook her head. 'Nothing like that. I have a couple of books of old postcards, if they'll be any use. What are you looking for? Historical pictures? Local, perhaps?'

She started to feel uneasy as he paused, almost staring into her with his slate grey eyes.

'A specific set,' he continued. 'A friend of mine had a box of photographs stolen so I'm checking to see if anyone on the market's been offered any.'

He had a foreign accent that she couldn't place. She sat as if in thought for a few seconds before shaking her head again.

'No, but I can keep an eye out if you give me a number?'

He smiled a thin lipped smile, but there was no warmth in it.

'Yes, here you are.' He handed her a piece of paper. 'If I don't answer, leave a message and put them to one side. I'll give you a good price.'

'But how will I know if they are the ones you want?'

'I'll take my chances. They are of far greater sentimental value to my friend than financial, so he's happy to pay more than they are worth. Don't forget to ring if you are offered any.'

Lyndsey put the paper into her pocket. 'Of course I will.'

'Thank you.'

He walked away and disappeared round Sammy's stall towards the rest of the market.

What a strange coincidence. He couldn't mean my parents' photos. They wouldn't be important to anyone other than me.

Mads checked her watch as she crossed the road. 6.50, and based on what Lyndsey had said this was about the time Barry had disappeared the day before. Walking towards Lyndsey's alcove, she watched dealers scurrying around stalls with their torches. Some exchanged brief greetings with each other, but most scanned in silence. She slowed as she neared Ranjit's pitch, taking in all the different textiles he had on display. She imagined the stall would be almost kaleidoscopic when the sun was out.

She stopped and ran her hand over one of the silky fabrics.

'Good morning, madam. You look like a discerning customer. Finest Indian silk at a price you will not believe.'

Mads picked up the corner and rubbed it together between her finger and thumb.

'Are you sure? This feels more like art silk to me.'

'Yes, indeed, finest Indian art silk. Would you like to see the full colour range?'

'Maybe later. I'm a reporter. I'm interested in some information on the man who was killed here yesterday.' She whipped out her pad and pen.

'Sorry, like I told the police, I saw nothing. With all the fabrics behind me I struggle to see what's going on back there.'

He indicated behind him and Mads looked at the hanging silks.

'From here, sure, but yours is the corner pitch. Doesn't it continue round?'

He nodded. 'It does, but I was here serving customers so saw nothing. It's rare that people approach from that direction until later.'

'You must have known the victim, though. What can you tell me about him?'

'Not much. The person you need to ask is the girl running the next stall. She was living with him.'

'I'll make a note of that, thanks. So what were your impressions of ... Barry was it?'

Ranjit scowled. 'He seemed OK, but he mixed with some dodgy people.'

'What do you mean?'

'He was mates with a group of right wing skinheads.

They used to turn up and chat to him here every so often.'

'Did they give you any trouble?'

'Nothing worth making a fuss over,' he said. 'The odd comment here and there, but their t-shirts and jacket patches didn't leave much room for doubt.'

'Was Barry like that too?' asked Mads.

'I don't think so. I asked him about them once and he said they were people he knew from school. Claimed he didn't know anything about their politics as he never discussed it with them. He only talked to them about music.'

'Sounds like a cop out to me.'

Ranjit shrugged. 'I suppose so, but you get used to it. Everyone's so full of their own problems, there's no time for anyone else's.'

'So you saw nothing suspicious?'

'No, nothing. Everything was normal until the scream. At that point I might as well have gone home. Loads of people wanting to gawk at what had happened but no one interested in buying anything.'

'So who do you think might have murdered Barry?'

'I wouldn't like to say. Lyndsey on the next stall knew him, and one of her knives was the murder weapon.'

'Do you think she did it?'

He shrugged. 'She doesn't seem the type, but who does? I can't imagine it was any of the other stallholders.

It's a bit neat, though, isn't it? She turns up here for the first time in years and within a couple of hours her ex is murdered with a knife from her stall. I can't help thinking that the police would have arrested her if there wasn't room for doubt.'

'Yes, you could be right.' She scribbled down her name and number on the bottom of the page and tore it off. 'If you remember anything, or hear anything relevant, please give me a call.'

Ranjit folded the piece of paper and put it into his back pocket.

'OK, but I don't expect I'm likely to hear much aside from rumours.'

Mads sauntered to the corner and turned into the alcove. It was still dark and the dim lighting did little to aid visibility. Taking a knife from Lyndsey's stall without being seen wouldn't be the most difficult job in the world. However, those exact conditions could also have enabled Lyndsey to sneak across and kill Barry.

Nobody from any of the stalls had noticed Mads' arrival. Granted, the end pitch was still taped off, as was Barry's, but it wasn't too much of a leap to imagine they had been busy the day before and not spotted anything unusual. She ambled up to Lyndsey.

'Hey, Lynds. How's it going?'

'I was wondering where you'd got to. What took you so long?'

'I'll fill you in later. Anything happened here I should know about?'

'Nothing special. Everyone's a bit subdued, or it might just be me. I can't help thinking most people think I killed Barry.'

'Oh don't be daft. Why would they think that?'

'I don't know, when I look up I catch them staring at me then they turn their heads away. I'm sure I never used to be that interesting.'

'Let them think what they want, we'll prove them wrong. Not that I imagine for a moment that they suspect you of murder. I bet they are looking at each other too. Even if they don't think they're guilty, they'll be assuming someone must know something. Like Maple Street from The Twilight Zone. Once something happens to shake people out of their comfort zone, they want to find some-one to blame.'

Lyndsey laughed. 'Maple Street? I hope it doesn't degenerate that much.'

'It's unlikely. I very much doubt aliens are behind Barry's murder.'

'So international hitmen, fine, but aliens would be a bit of a stretch?'

'Trust me on this, Lynds. I'm a detective.'

Mads managed to keep a straight face for a few seconds then both her and Lyndsey tried to stifle their laughter with their hands as best they could.

'Shush, you'll blow your cover.'

'Yes, I'd better crack on.'

'Tell Bob and Jools you were mates with me at the paper. They'll be more likely to open up to you if they think you're on my side.'

'Will do. I'll catch you later.'

Mads walked to the next stall and gaped in amazement at all the mirrors. If she wasn't careful she could end up spending a small fortune.

'Mornin' love. Anything here you like or were you looking for something specific?'

'Goodness, Bob, let the poor girl get her bearings. You'll be scaring her off.'

Mads smiled. 'Don't tempt me. I'm a great lover of mirrors. Too much so.'

'A house isn't a home without mirrors, that's what I always say,' said Jools.

'I'm guessing you're Jools, and you must be Bob,' she said. 'I used to work with Lyndsey at the paper and she told me I should talk to you both. I'm investigating yesterday's murder.'

'Oh, really?' asked Bob, looking across at Lyndsey. Out of the corner of her eye, Mads saw her smile and give him a thumbs-up.

'Yes, I asked my editor to put me on the story because I can't believe she had anything to do with it.'

'No, she was at the food van when Barry disappeared.'

'So someone could have taken the knife while she was gone?'

'I didn't see anyone approach her pitch, and I had half an eye on it in case she got a customer.'

Mads glanced towards Lyndsey.

'Would you, though? You've not got a perfect view from here due to the mirrors, and with the dealers flitting in and out with their torches it might be difficult to make someone out unless they came up to the stall and waited.'

'Yes, we figure someone grabbed it and scooted off straight away. Still, I don't suppose you'd hang around, would you?'

'You didn't see anything or anybody unusual?'

'There was a big guy arguing with Barry, but he arrived before Lyndsey went for food so I doubt he took it. Aside from that, it was the usual stream of dealers looking for new items and bargains.'

'How about the man who was browsing after she got back?' said Jools. 'What if he'd disabled Barry somehow, bundled him into the wardrobe and took the knife to finish him off?'

'Sounds a bit far fetched to me,' said Bob, 'but still better than the police's theory that me or Lyndsey did it.'

'What did he look like?' asked Mads.

'I couldn't say,' said Jools, 'but Lyndsey took her toastie and sat there while he browsed, so she's the best person to ask.'

'So what did you both think of Barry?'

There was a brief pause before Jools answered.

'I never took to him. He was too cocky and full of himself. Lyndsey liked him though, so there much have been something about him.'

'Yes,' said Mads. 'I'm getting the impression he could be something of a charmer when he wanted to be. How about you, Bob?'

'I thought he was OK, until yesterday.'

'What happened to make you change your mind? And while I think of it, why do you think the police have you on the suspect list?'

Jools raised her eyebrows and a sheepish expression crossed his face.

'You might as well tell her, Bob. It speaks for Barry's character if nothing else.'

'I guess, but off the record, yeah? I don't want to read

about it in the newspaper.'

Mads nodded and made a zipping motion across her lips.

'I met him in the pub a couple of weeks ago and he said he needed some money for Lyndsey's birthday surprise so I lent him some. Yesterday I found out that her birthday isn't until December.'

'Which he'd have known at the time if he hadn't been drunk.'

'I'll be paying for that until her actual birthday,' said Bob, smiling.

'He also underestimates my stamina,' said Jools with a wry smile of her own.

Mads laughed. 'So how much did you lend him?'

'£250. Nothing worth killing him for, if that's what you're thinking.'

'No, I wasn't. Getting paid by a corpse must be a struggle.'

'What a shame the Inspector isn't as logical as you. He thought being owed money was a solid motive.'

'Though he suspects Lyndsey too,' said Jools, 'so I'm not sure he's much of an oracle.'

Mads made some notes.

'So who do you think did it?'

'No idea,' said Bob. 'I wish we did.'

Jools nodded in agreement. 'We were up half the night picking over every detail we could remember but came up empty. Maybe you'll manage to uncover something we missed. Fresh pair of eyes syndrome.'

'I hope you're right. Let me give you my number, just in case something comes to you. Anything else you can think of before I go?'

'No, but please don't tell Lynds about the money,' said Bob. 'I wouldn't want her feeling guilty that Barry used her name to con me.'

Mads winked at him. 'Don't you worry, it'll be our little secret.'

She sauntered back to Lyndsey.

'They said someone approached your stall after you got back from the food van?'

'Oh yes. He was browsing through the programmes. Barry had disappeared by then.'

'But we don't know the exact timeline. What if he grabbed a knife and browsed for a while to allay suspicion. Afterwards, having arranged to meet Barry behind his stall for a drug deal ...'

'What drug deal? Where did that come from?'

'... or something else just as shady. He kills him, takes whatever he wanted and stashes the body. All I'm saying is, what if Barry wasn't killed when he disappeared. What if it happened a bit later?'

Lyndsey was still wide-eyed. 'Why do you think he was dealing drugs?'

Mads reached out and touched the top of Lyndsey's arm to try to relax her.

'I don't—but it's possible. I have the feeling he was involved in something you haven't got a Scooby about, and whatever it was there's a good chance it could lead us to the killer.'

19

As Mads walked away, Lyndsey made her way through the mirrors.

'She's a friend of yours?' asked Bob as she approached.

'Yes, we first met at university. Did she manage to stir any memories?'

'Nothing of any use, we brainstormed yesterday morning a thousand times between the two of us last night, and the whole affair is a complete mystery.'

'Isn't everything quiet, without the music in the background,' said Jools. 'I never used to realise it was there, until now when it's missing.'

'I thought that earlier. There's an eerie silence hanging over the place. So you didn't suggest to her that Barry might be involved with anything illegal?'

Bob and Jools stared at her. 'Why, was he?' asked Bob.

'Not that I'm aware, but Mads made a comment just

now. I was wondering if you said anything or if it was just a figment of her overactive imagination.'

'I don't think she got anything from us. Like I said, we're both clueless where it comes to motives for killing Barry. Wouldn't you have known if he was up to anything?'

'I'd like to think so, but I'm so full of doubt at the moment, I'm not sure of anything.'

'You take a few deep breaths and relax. Everything will come good, you'll see.'

'I hope so. While i think of it, how well did you know my parents?'

Bob raised his eyebrows. 'Not at all, we never met them. Why do you ask?'

Lyndsey shrugged. 'Just curious. With Barry being murdered, it got me thinking about how little I know about them as people.'

'We knew Bert from the old market before this one opened. He's the man to ask.'

'Yes, but all his stories are coated with a rose-tinted veneer. It would be interesting to hear another perspective not warped by his parental vision or my childhood memories.'

'Sorry, you must know far more than we do.' He paused for a few seconds. 'What type of stall do you think will open in Barry's old pitch. Might make a change to have something like vases and pottery to complement the mirrors, furniture and art. What do you think, Jools?'

'That would be good, but it's not our decision. I sometimes wonder at the policies in the office, though. They don't put similar stalls too close together, but I often think it might be better to group all the mirror sellers in the same alcove, and so on. Sure we'd be competing, but everyone who wanted mirrors would know where to come so we could attract more trade collectively.'

'Like takeaway shops always cluster on High Streets?' asked Lyndsey.

'Yes, that sort of thing.'

'I'm happy as it is,' said Bob. 'Not sure market buyers are the same kind of customer. Most don't have a clue what they want until they see something they like, so being surrounded by complementary products might work best. Food shopping is a different animal.'

'Perhaps, I was just thinking that all the fruit and veg stalls are clustered together, but like you say, it's not the same. No one wants to be browsing the entire market with a sack of spuds on their shoulder.'

'Are you listening, Lynds? That could be the closest Jools has ever come to admitting I'm right about something.'

Lyndsey smiled. 'I didn't hear a thing. Catch you later.'

She walked back to her stall and sat down again. Once she was settled, Bob pulled out his phone and made a call. It was answered after a couple of rings.

'Hi.'

'Hey, it might be nothing, but you remember you asked me ages ago to tell you if Lyndsey asked about her parents?'

'Yes.'

'Well, she just did. It could be that yesterday has her unsettled, but I thought I'd tell you.'

'Thanks, no one out of the ordinary hanging around?'

'Not that we've noticed.'

'OK, well keep an eye out.'

'Of course, we'll let you know if anything strange happens. Bye.'

20

As she walked across to Mary's stall, Mads wondered how anyone could hang these paintings on their walls without having nightmares. The bright, bold colours were overwhelming at first, though an enormous representation of what she took to be the Eye of Sauron stood out, if only because it had pride of place in the centre of the display. Only when she got closer did the realisation dawn on her that, eww, that was no Eye of Sauron. As she tried to eradicate the image from her mind, her phone rang and she glanced at the screen before answering it.

'Nigel, what can I do for you?'

'Hi Mads. Can you transfer some money for me, please? I need a quarter million in account one. Try number four, if not enough in there move it from account five instead.'

'OK, but it won't be for a couple of hours. I'm not

at home.'

'No problem, it just needs to be there by the morning. I would do it myself but the hotel internet's flaky and I don't trust public internet for banking.'

Mads flipped a few pages over in the pad and scribbled down the details.

'I'll do it when I get back. How are you?'

'Good, yourself? I should be home in a couple of weeks time. Just for a day or two, before jetting off to South America.'

'I'll look forward to it. I understand Good Housekeeping magazine now recommend that married couples are in the same country for at least a day or two a month.'

'Now now, don't be sarky. It's only for another couple of years.'

'I know. It doesn't make it any easier though.'

'It'll be worth the wait, we're past the halfway point. I must go and grab some breakfast. Speak to you when I get back, if not before.'

'See you soon.'

She put the phone back in her pocket and continued towards Mary's stall. She was sitting on a chair and smiled as Mads approached.

'Hi'

'Hi, I'm a reporter with the local paper and wondered if you could spare a couple of minutes to talk about the murder.'

Mary shrugged. 'Sure, but I didn't really see anything.'

Mads studied the small half-stall that Mary shared with Martin, self-contained in its tent.

'You've built yourself a cosy little nest here.'

'When you share a space it's important to create a defined boundary else it can cause bad feelings. It's a nuisance putting it up on Saturday morning and taking it down Sunday, but it gives me a roof too so no panicking at the first sign of rain.'

'Why do you and Martin share? Have you known each other long?'

'No, it was a bit of luck. The market had advertised pitches and we turned up at the office the same time. As neither of us could comfortably afford the cost of a full stall, we talked them into giving us both a contract for half.'

'And it's all worked out?'

'Yes, we get along fine. Books and art complement each other too, so it's a win-win.'

'So where was the body found? Just the other side of your wall?'

'Yes, right behind me. I almost fell off my chair, the scream was so piercing.'

'You didn't hear anything before that? No struggle or noises when the body was put into the wardrobe?'

'Nothing, really. Barry had his music playing so it must have covered up anything else.'

'Did he play it loud?'

'I wouldn't say so, but first thing in the morning before the sun rises everything sounds louder. Not many people around to deaden it, I suppose.'

Mads glanced over her shoulder towards Lyndsey's stall. 'There's a perfect view of the stalls across the way from here. Did you see anyone or anything suspicious yesterday morning?'

'Like what?'

'Whoever took the knife?'

'Nothing like that, though I wasn't really paying attention. Once I've laid out my paintings I just sit here reading.'

'Did you get on well with Barry?'

Mary shrugged. 'Yes, not that well, though. Just to say hello to.'

'He didn't try to hit on you?'

'Haha, of course. I'd have been insulted if he hadn't, given that he flirted with every woman he met who had a pulse, but I wasn't interested.'

'How did he take being rejected?'

'He laughed, said he'd wear me down in the end. Give him his due, he never gave up. Every few weeks for the last couple of years he'd try his luck and I'd reject him again. I think he enjoyed the challenge.'

Mads looked around the stall again and noticed the walls were hanging loose so not connected at the back corners.

'Thanks for your time. Would you mind if I took a quick peek behind the tent?'

'Carry on, but it's the same as the other stalls.'

'I'm sure, but I want to get a feel for how Barry would get from his stall to the wardrobe.'

Mary shrugged and went back to her book. Mads followed a narrow rat run between the easels to the back left corner and lifted the back flap so she could get through. To her disappointment, everything was the same as behind the other stalls. A blue box van was parked about a metre back from the tent. The route between Barry's pitch and the furniture stall was clear. He could have walked or been dragged across without disturbing anyone. There were no bloodstains though, and if she'd learnt anything from television it was that stabbing someone to death resulted in plenty of blood. She made her way to the police tape and CSI tent. There was a half metre gap between Mary's tent and this one, so she edged her way along, trying to sneak a quick peek inside. Not until she was two metres or so in front of Mary's stall, did she reach the corner of the CSI tent and the only face with a door.

She shuffled forward a little, leaning across to try to peer through a small plastic window. She crept a little farther, hoping the tape wouldn't snap, when the tent flap whipped open and out strode a body dressed like there had been a nuclear spill.

'Sorry, madam. We don't set all this up as an elaborate game, you're meant to stay the other side.'

'Well, I am, sort of,' said Mads, backing up so the tape wasn't as stretched. 'I'm studying forensics at University and thought it would be interesting to get a glimpse of a real crime scene.' She cocked her head to the side and batted her eyelashes. 'I don't suppose ...'

'Student, huh? Then shouldn't you know better?'

Mads took her purse from her pocket and mentally high-fived herself for never clearing it out. Right at the back she found her old ID card that, for reasons of university economy, was devoid of any dates.

'See!' she said, brandishing it in front of him and resting her right hand on his upper arm. She had expected the coverall to feel artificial, like plastic, but it was soft to the touch as if made from multiple layers of net curtains.

'Very good, though my emphasis was on the part

where you should know better.'

Mads stuck her bottom lip out.

'Can't I take a quick peek through the flap? I won't compromise anything.'

His eyes creased a little, as if he was smiling under his face mask. 'I'm just finishing up and the guys will be along at three to break everything down. If you come back about two o'clock I'll let you have a gander. How does that sound?'

'You're a star,' said Mads, putting her student card away and flashing him her best smile. 'I'll be back at two.'

He disappeared through the flap and she made her way back between the two tents. That was a turn up, and she was excited to study a real crime scene, as the butter-flies dancing in her belly were testament to.

Lyndsey pulled a notepad and a phone from her pocket. Although she couldn't help Mads with the direct questioning, the least she could do was to collect some background information on the stallholders. She navigated to the market's website and found the weekend map. After scrolling to their alcove, she clicked on the icon for Sammy's stall.

A page loaded, showing her his name, business contact details and links to his website and eBay store. She noted down his information and set about searching through his site. After five minutes on there and eBay, she concluded he might be telling the truth regarding his animal remains. Copies of the certificates of authenticity and ethicality for the items were displayed online. It didn't mean he wasn't a murderer, but it made her feel a little better about his merchandise.

She moved on to Martin and found he ran a second hand book store on eBay. His site encouraged people to bring their used books along to the market to exchange them on a two for one basis or to negotiate a price if they wanted to sell. Online he offered an extensive range of fiction and non-fiction though from what she could see, the selection he'd brought today was far smaller.

In contrast, Mary looked as if she was displaying everything she had. Her website had many more paintings displayed, but many were marked as sold with instructions to visit her eBay or Etsy stores to buy prints instead. She also had a calendar showing when her work would be exhibited at Art Centres and Galleries around the UK. While her art wasn't to Lyndsey's taste, others must disagree as her agenda was busy.

She continued around the alcove for completeness, though the only other new thing she learnt was that Ranjit also owned a clothing factory in Southall connected to a shop run by his wife.

She put the notepad back into her pocket, feeling a little deflated. While it would have been too much to hope for to discover that someone had been a knife-thrower in a circus or had a record of violent crime, she'd hoped to unearth something interesting.

Mads decided to approach Martin's stall from behind, if only to get a different view of Barry's old space. She walked behind Mary's tent and around the corner to found him sitting with his back to her, reading a book. She waited until she was a metre from him before announcing her arrival.

'Hi, you must be Martin.'

He jumped in his seat and turned to face her.

'Sorry about that, I'm a local reporter. I wondered if you had a few minutes to answer some questions.'

He swivelled his head towards the market, as if begging a customer to appear, but none did.

'I suppose so. I'm guessing it's about Barry?'

'Yes, you must have known him well, being on the next stall?'

'No, I'd say hello, but he wasn't the sort of person I'd

be friends with. A bit too full of himself.'

Mads looked at the boxes he had on display.

'Nice little set up you have here. Do you sell much?'

'Most of my business is online. The best thing with the market is that I can try to shift books that aren't getting much interest on the Internet. I offer a trading system, so if people bring me two I don't have, I'll exchange them for one of mine. Sometimes more if they have something interesting. It keeps the stock rotating.'

'What a good idea. I must dig out a few of my old books and swap with you some time. Did you see anything that morning? You have a good view of the stall the knife came from.'

'Nothing. It was still gloomy and I box everything at home ready to put on display, so it doesn't take me long to set up. Once that's done I sit here and read until I have customers.'

'Do you remember a big man arguing with Barry?'

He thought for a moment. 'Yes, but I couldn't hear what they were saying over the music. I think he had dark hair, but I'm not sure. I didn't pay attention. He was still OK when the guy walked off, though.'

'You're sure on that?'

'No doubt about it. Barry swore when he left. Not at him, just out of frustration. Then pulled his phone out and called someone.'

'What then?'

'Nothing, I never saw him again. Not alive.'

Mads pointed towards the back of the pitch.

'Is that your van or Mary's?'

'My brother's. He lets us use it at weekends to ferry the stock back and forth.'

'That's good of him. So are you and Mary a couple?'

'No, just friends.' His tone and the way his eyes glanced down at the floor when he spoke gave Mads the impression he wasn't content with being Mary's friend.

'So, who do you think the murderer might be?'

He shrugged. 'No idea. That Lyndsey is the obvious suspect.'

'Why do you say that?'

'Well, it was her knife and rumour has it she split up with Barry last week.'

'But you didn't see her do anything suspicious?'

'No, but she was missing from her pitch when he disappeared.'

'OK, thanks for your time. If you hear or remember anything could you give me a call?' She handed him her number.

'No problem.'

He folded the strip of paper into his jacket pocket.

Mads ducked under his stall flaps and as an afterthought strolled back to where Mary was sitting.

'Hey, I forgot to give you my details, in case you remember anything that might be useful,' she said, handing it over.

'Thanks. Any luck yet?'

'No one's seen anything. It's like investigating a gunfight in South Newark.'

'I understand what you mean. Sorry I can't be more help.'

'You can't think of anyone here who might have wanted Barry dead?'

'No, I wouldn't like to think anybody from the market was capable of such a thing. Not those from our cluster. That would be creepy.'

'Yes, I suppose it would. Thanks for the chat, and don't forget to ring if anything comes to mind.'

'Will do.'

Mads walked off in the direction of Sammy's stall as Mary's attention drifted back to her book. Martin watched as she passed and she smiled at him. Sammy was busy with a couple of customers, so she decided to talk to the stallholders who backed onto Barry's pitch. None of them had any useful information, so she followed her nose to the catering van. She checked her watch as she joined the queue. Eight-forty. She figured it was late enough by now and dialled Sharon's number. After four or five rings, it was answered.

'Hello?'

'Hi, is that Sharon?'

'Yeah, who's this.'

'My name's Mads, I'm a reporter and I wondered if we could have a quick chat about Barry.'

There was a pause.

'Why, what's he done?'

Oh, this is awkward.

'Could we meet for breakfast and I'll fill you in? I only need some background on him. I'm buying, of course.'

Sharon paused again.

'Breakfast's a bit soon. How about lunch?'

Mads smiled to herself. 'I can manage that. Where would be best for you?'

'Do you know The Intern in Isleworth? I can be there about half-twelve.'

'That will be perfect. How will I know you?'

'I'll wait outside the bar door. The first one you reach after you cross Mill Bridge.'

'OK, I'll look forward to meeting you at twelve-thirty.'

She hung up and glanced around. A few people sat

around the metal tables in conversation but she couldn't pick out anything they were saying. She doubted it mattered. Even if they were discussing the murder they were likelier to be exchanging wild theories rather than hard evidence. She reached the front of the queue and ordered a baked bean toastie and two black teas.

So far this morning seemed a waste of time, apart from the girls in the café. She doubted Sammy was going to be any more help than the others had been. Still, she reasoned, if you shake the bushes perhaps the guilty party will panic and bolt. Her order arrived and she slipped the toastie into her pocket and carried the two teas back. Sammy was customer-free so she headed for his stall and found a space to put the drinks down.

'Hi.'

'Hello there. The morning's taken a turn for the better. Pretty ladies don't bring me coffee every day.' He smiled a bright white smile at her.

Mads laughed. 'No, sorry. That one's for my mate.'

'Just my luck. So, what can I do for you? Are you looking for a slice of Africa to brighten up your walls?'

She wrinkled her nose up at the skulls and stuffed heads. 'No, too gruesome for my taste. I wouldn't be able to sleep at night.'

'None of my stock is from poachers. They all died

natural deaths and I have certificates to prove it. My uncle has a licence to collect skulls and pelts from the Serengeti National Park. Once the scavengers eat their fill, he picks up the remains and sends some over to me. Everything's legal and above board.'

She raised her hands to him in a "whoa, hold your horses" gesture.

'From the Serengeti? Whereabouts is that? Geography was never my strong suit.'

'Tanzania, you should visit one day. It's a beautiful country.'

Mads gave him a smile and nodded towards a wall mat behind him.

'It must be for that tiger to have swum all the way from India for the pleasure of dying there. If I had that kind of motivation, who knows what I could manage in a day.'

Sammy glanced round and threw his hands up. 'Lady, you're sharp. Fair enough, the tiger skin I picked up from one of the other stalls a few weeks ago so I don't know its history. I could tell you where I got it though, if you want to check. I have nothing to hide.'

'No pun intended, right?'

Sammy laughed again. 'You're too smart for me. What can I help you with, if you're not after any of my beautiful animals?'

'I'm a reporter and wondered if you could tell me anything about Barry?'

Sammy's smile disappeared. 'What about him?'

'Judging by your reaction you didn't get on.'

Sammy shrugged. 'We did once, but he ripped me off. Now he's dead I'll never see my money.'

'How so?'

'I had a collection of records I wanted to sell and he promised to get me the best price. They were worth a few hundred, I reckon. I gave them to him, then all I got back was excuses and promises.'

'That sucks.'

'Yeah, right? And if your thought process is like that detective's, no I didn't kill him during an argument. If I had, I would at least have taken his money.'

'Yes, that would make sense. Did you see anything suspicious, or have any idea who did it?'

'No, I'm facing away from his pitch and the gazelles block my view.' He pointed at some pelts lining the back wall of his stall. 'Maybe somebody had less patience than me. I doubt I was the only person he's stiffed over the years.'

'You don't know of anyone else though?'

'I wouldn't have given him my records in the first

place if I had. Let's face it, no one decides it's a great plan to only screw over the six foot four black guy. I must be part of a pattern, somewhere along the way.'

They laughed.

'Let me give you my number, in case you think of anything.' Mads tore off another strip of paper and handed it to Sammy.

'I'll keep my ear to the ground for you, but no one around here knows anything from what I can gather.'

'That's the impression I'm getting.' She picked up the teas. 'Thanks for your time.'

'No problem, I hope I'll see you again.' He flashed her another broad smile.

She walked across to Lyndsey and put the drinks down.

'Thanks. How is it going?'

'No one's confessed yet.' She took the paper bag from her pocket and handed it over. 'Here, I got you a toastie.'

'Ugh, not sure I can eat anything after that breakfast.'

'I'm sure you'll manage by the time it cools down. It's difficult to tell what I've got so far. Everyone claims to have heard and seen nothing. We can analyse everything later on. Speaking of which, are we going to talk to the people who run the furniture stall? Their pitch is best placed to notice anything and everything that goes on.'

'Good idea. I'll check whether Bob has their home address. If so, we can pop over this afternoon.'

'Sounds good. I need to get a few bits done, but I'll be back for two. I managed to talk the CSI cop in the hazmat suit to let me poke my nose around inside the crime tent before they break it all down.'

'How did you manage that?'

'I have my ways. He thinks I'm a forensics student though, so don't blow it for me.'

Lyndsey smiled. 'I'll do my best to resist outing your fake reporter status, don't you worry. See you about two.'

23

Mads caught a bus back home and made a mug of tea. While the kettle boiled, she opened up the laptop and transferred Nigel's money across. Once that was done, she sat down and scanned through her notes from the morning. She couldn't imagine for a moment that no one had seen or heard anything out of the ordinary yesterday. To make matters worse, she was sure that everyone was being less than truthful about something. Not that that made them guilty, after all, she was lying about being a journalist and that didn't make her a murderer either.

At 11.30, she headed off to catch a bus to Isleworth. Marketing types were all too hurried to sell you the dream of the freedom of the road, but she doubted any of them lived in London. They also forgot to mention the tyranny of the controlled parking zone that made it impossible to park without knowing an area like the back of your hand.

Buses and trains were far more civilised, until you needed to get out of the city. Plus, bonus points if you managed to grab a front seat upstairs so you could play driver, something she had never tired of since she had first moved to London.

Mads got off the bus just past the hospital and cut through an alleyway towards The Intern. It was lovely with all the trees overhead, but she imagined it would be scary at night. She shuddered, remembering back to her adventure along the Thames towpath.

The alley finished by Mill Bridge, and she smiled at the sound of the water bubbling away to her right. She wished she had seen Isleworth Village before it had been turned into a stream of gated communities. The original buildings must have been so charming and full of character.

She turned left, away from the bridge and as she rounded a corner saw a woman in her early twenties standing outside the door to The Intern. She had dark brown hair to her shoulders and would be attractive if not for the bags under her eyes and sullen expression on her face.

'Hi, are you Sharon?'

'Yeah.'

'I'm Mads. Shall we go in?'

They entered the pub and she took in the décor.

The floor was wooden and in front of them was a television showing football with the sound turned down. They turned left and made their way between a row of bar stools and tables where they passed another silent television. This one was mounted high on the wall and tuned to the same channel. Music that Mads had never heard before but assumed to be recent chart hits played through the speakers positioned through the pub.

They left the football den and walked through to another area. This was a pleasant, old style bar with tables placed in alcoves along the wall. An oar was hanging on the lintel that ran across the ceiling printed with the moniker, "Dartmouth Boat Club 1902". Through the window she could see the River Thames flowing past and she imagined this would be a lovely pub to come for a drink in the summer when the weather would be amenable to sitting outside.

'Where do you want to sit?' asked Mads.

'Here all right?' asked Sharon as she sat herself down facing the bar with her back to the window.

'Works for me. What can I get you to drink?'

'Lager and lime, please.'

'No problem, how about food?'

Sharon plucked a menu from a stand on the table and browsed its contents.

'The beef roast, and this is table 7,' she said, pointing at the number.

Mads went to the bar and glanced at a menu while a barman poured the lager and lime and a pint of 1730. The vegetarian fish and chips sounded great, but like most of the fare on offer wasn't vegan. She plumped for a side order of fries, took the beers to the table and sat down.

'Blimey, I only expected an half.'

'Sorry, I never understood the concept of halves. You only end up going to the bar twice as often. So, tell me about Barry.'

'What's he done first? I don't want to get him into trouble, even if he is a bastard.'

Mads debated with herself how to handle this. Should she lie and say he's missing? Try to soften the blow somehow? She decided to be direct.

'He was murdered at the market yesterday morning. Someone stabbed him to death with an old knife.'

Sharon's eyes opened like saucers along with her mouth for a few moments, then her face took on a strange, calm. She looked down at the table.

'Good, I hope he suffered.'

Mads stayed quiet. As if realising what she had just said, Sharon jerked her head up looking shocked.

'It wasn't me, though. I was at home all day yesterday,

honest.'

Mads smiled. 'I believe you. I wanted to talk to you so I could collect some background information on him, that's all. The more I find out about Barry, the better chance I stand of catching who murdered him.'

'Why do you care? It's the police's job to find who-ever killed him.'

'At the moment they think my friend was involved, and I want to prove them wrong because she didn't do it.'

'Was she another girl he spun a line to?'

'Yes, I think she was, but she wouldn't kill him. That I'm sure of.'

Sharon nodded and stared at the table deep in thought.

'At the risk of sounding like the most gullible idiot in the area, I'm guessing he didn't live with his sick mother, did he?'

Mads didn't reply.

'Thought not, that explains why we could never go back to his place. How could I be so stupid?'

'Don't blame yourself. More people are decent than not, and if you push them all away in case they can't be trusted, you'll miss out on the good ones. We've all come across a Barry or two, trust me.'

They fell quiet as the barman came across to deliver their food. 'Enjoy,' he said. 'Anything else I can get you?'

'No thanks,' said Mads.

He went back to the bar and they both started eating.

'So, what can you tell me about him?'

Sharon shrugged. 'You might know more about him than I do. I'm beginning to wonder if his name really was Barry.'

'Ignore what he told you. Where did you go? Who else did you meet when you were with him?'

Sharon chewed as she thought.

'We didn't do much. He came round mine when I wasn't working and my parents were out. Other than that we went down The Polar in Hounslow. His mates used to hang out there, so we'd have a few drinks and play pool on Monday, Tuesday and Wednesday. He said the home help didn't work Friday through Sunday so he had to be with his mum and I've no idea what he got up to Thursdays. We never stayed out late. I was always home by nine or so.'

'You can't remember him having an argument with anyone?'

'Nothing like that. He got on with everybody.'

'So why did you break up?'

Sharon chewed in silence for a few seconds while studying her plate as if it was the most interesting piece of china she'd ever seen.

'I fell pregnant but it turned out Barry wasn't much

of a family man.'

Mads stayed quiet, waiting to see if she would expand on that but she didn't.

'Are you still ...?'

'No, I had an accident and lost it. I'm just getting over everything.'

Mads decided not to push her any further on the 'accident'. Jacks and Shirl had filled her in on what happened and there was nothing to be gained from causing Sharon any more anguish. They had both finished eating and Mads glanced at her watch. It was nearly half past one.

'I must be going in a moment,' she said. 'Do you want another drink before I do?'

'No, thanks. Hope you find whoever killed him. I wish I could be more help.'

After saying their goodbyes, Mads arrived at the bus stop just as the bus was rounding the corner so got to the market in good time. As she neared the CSI tent a man standing outside it smiled at her. He had short, brown hair styled in a side parting and a trim beard and moustache. He was dressed in jeans and a red polo shirt beneath a light blue woollen sweater.

'Early, I see. My name's Steve. Come through.'

She ducked under the police tape.

'I'm Mads,' she said. 'I almost didn't recognise you

without your spacesuit.'

'Ha, I'm pleased to be out of it. You wouldn't believe how hot you get in one of those things after a while. After you.'

He lifted the tent flap and she felt his hand in the small of her back as he guided her through. After her nervous anticipation, the reality was something of a let down. Seeing a wardrobe, she made her way towards it.

'So this is what he fell out of?' she asked, though the dried blood on the concrete rather answered the question for her. 'Any fingerprints?'

'Some, but they are being analysed back at base. They most likely belong to the stallholders and the woman who discovered the body.'

Mads moved behind the wardrobe where a larger bloodstain was visible.

'I'm guessing this was where he was stabbed? And judging by the spatter, he was facing this way,' she said indicating behind her towards the market.

'Very good. He was unlucky, single stab wound on his right side, severing an artery. That's an unusual thing to happen. Anything else you notice?'

Mads squatted down and studied the bloodstain closer. 'I'd expect the spatter to be wider, or is that due to the knife not being pulled out?'

'No, we think the killer blocked the path of the blood so likely caught a fair amount on their clothes.'

'That must be useful to know.'

'Only if we find it. If we'd noticed someone wearing blood-soaked clothing yesterday it would be game over, but life is rarely that kind. It will add to the weight of evidence after we catch the murderer.'

Mads followed the blood trail while making sure not to tread on it, 'So the killer dragged the body round here, opened the wardrobe and shoved him in before closing the door again.'

'That's fairly certain. They wiped the handle, or wore gloves, not unreasonable on an early October morning. They also took care not to make any footprints in the blood as that would have proved useful.'

She looked at the door. 'Why leave the key? If they had locked the door and taken it with them, the body might have been discovered far later?'

'The door was unlocked and it was taped to the base of the wardrobe. Whoever it was can't have realised, else it would have made sense to take it with them, as you say. We put it in the door so we can lock it to keep cross contamination to a minimum.'

'It's unlikely to have been premeditated, wouldn't you say? Public place, murder weapon taken from a nearby stall, no post-kill strategy.'

Steve shrugged. 'From first impressions it looks that way, but I don't know what other evidence has been uncovered from the body and knife. I know it appears to be a big tent, but we've covered all the interesting bits if you're done?'

'Of course, I wouldn't want to get you into any trouble. How come you're the only one here? I expected a team.'

Steve laughed. 'You only have teams on the television. In real life it's almost always just one CSI operative with maybe a uniform on guard outside, depending on the area and the crime.' They walked towards the exit. 'If you're free we could meet for a drink later if you want to learn more about forensics?'

'I'd love to but I'm not sure what my husband has planned for this evening,' she said, waggling her ring finger at him.

'Ouch, well I hope you got something out of this and good luck with your studies.'

Mads leant in and kissed him on the cheek. 'Thanks, Steve, you're a sweetheart.'

She left and ducked under the police tape. Lyndsey was leaning against the van waiting for her. Bob and Jools were packing away the last of their mirrors, and over her shoulder Martin and Mary were taking the tent down from her pitch. She opened the door and hopped in as Lyndsey climbed into the driver's side. They slammed the doors shut together.

'So how did everything go, Sherlock?'

'Give me a couple of minutes.' Mads took the notebook from her pocket and flicked to a new page where she made a sketch. 'I needed to draw that while the scene was fresh in my mind. I thought it might look suspicious if I whipped my phone out and took photos.'

Lyndsey started the van and backed out. 'How did you manage to worm your way into the tent of death?'

'I had a bit of luck. I think poor Steve fancied me and as they'll be breaking everything down in an hour or so, he saw a chance to impress me without compromising anything. He was sweet, though, maybe I could introduce you both?'

'Don't you dare. I have enough problems at the moment without taking on your cast-offs.' She waved to Bob and Jools before heading off. 'So what did you find out?'

'Did you find out the furniture people's address? If we talk to them first, we can sort through everything over dinner.'

'No, Bob doesn't know where they live. I know where

their shop is, though, so we can visit them in Richmond tomorrow morning if you're free.'

'No problem. What did Barry do on Thursday nights?'

'That was his boys' night out. He went to The Polar with his mates.'

'In that case we should go to The Polar for a drink.'

Lyndsey shuddered. 'Ugh, why?'

'We need to find out what Barry really did every Thursday.'

Lyndsey drove back in silence, but no sooner had she parked the van in the garage and switched the engine off, she turned towards Mads.

'What do you mean, what he did? And what was with the drugs comment earlier? What do you know that I don't?'

'The only sure thing is that Barry lied to you. Why, and to what extent I'm not sure, but we need to find out if we're going to get to the bottom of this.'

'What did he lie about?'

Mads paused for a moment before opting to come straight out with it.

'There's at least one girl who thinks she was his girl-friend until they split up a couple of months ago. I've not uncovered any others, but it wouldn't surprise me if there are more.'

'Who? ... How? ... Ugh, ignore me, after Candy I don't know why I'm surprised. What else?'

'On top of that he owes people money. I'm not sure why or how much in total, but I'm guessing he never told you. Now, you didn't kill him, and I'm sure his other ex is innocent. I'm also certain it wasn't the people he owed, at least not those I've met, so we need to dig further.'

Lyndsey was staring at her with her mouth agape, as if in a daze. Mads put her arm around her shoulders.

'Hey, come on. I didn't want to tell you all that but you're going to hear it sometime. It's better coming from me than from the press or the police.'

'I know. It's just ... it's as if I never knew him at all. Are you sure about all this?'

Mads' silence spoke volumes. Lyndsey turned her head and sat still for a couple of seconds before opening the door.

'Yes, of course you are. Come on, let's take the cash indoors then we can set about finding out more about the mysterious world of Barry.'

'Are you sure you're OK?'

Lyndsey nodded. 'Yes, I want to find out who killed him, but I'm not sure whether I most want to get the police off my back or buy the killer a drink. Who did he owe money to?'

'I promised I wouldn't say. I think they are embarrassed that he conned them.'

'But I could try to pay them back.'

'You'll do nothing of the kind. They don't hold you responsible and you shouldn't feel guilty. He didn't just have you fooled. You're not to blame for any of this mess.'

Lyndsey nodded and climbed out. She leant back in to pick up the cash box and ledger from beneath the seat. 'Mads.'

Mads raised her eyebrow.

'Thanks.'

They carried the stock into the back room. Once that was done, she went through to the lounge.

'Hi, Grandad. Here's the money and the ledger. Sold a few programmes, and also got a list from a woman who wanted a quote for the lot. I got the impression she wants them out of her house more than to profit from them. Here you go.'

'Thanks, love. Did you manage to resist killing anyone today?'

She felt her cheeks go red. 'Oh don't, do you think I could do anything like that? Sorry I didn't say anything, I was in a rush and didn't want you to worry.'

'Don't you mind me, if you've got problems, tell me. You don't reach my age without knowing people who can help out in most situations.'

'I gave the police a statement and they kept my clothes for forensic tests. As I didn't kill him they won't find anything and can concentrate on finding who did do it. That's how the system works, isn't it?'

He smiled. 'It's how it should work, but hundreds of innocent people in prison would tell you otherwise. I'm just saying, keep me in the loop. So nothing else happened today, a normal quiet Sunday?'

She thought about the man asking about photographs and decided he wasn't important. 'Nothing out of the ordinary. I'm going out with Mads again. I doubt we'll be too late.'

'I thought you came in with someone. Where's she hiding, I haven't seen her in years?'

Mads walked through from the kitchen.

'Hi Bert. You're looking well.'

He gave her a hug. 'Mads, you look prettier every time I cast my eyes on you. If ever you want to replace that husband of yours, don't forget I'm still single.'

She laughed. 'As tempting as that sounds, I'm not sure my ego could handle Lyndsey calling me Granny.'

'Is it safe to leave you two alone for a couple of minutes while I change?' asked Lyndsey.

'You'd better hurry,' said Bert, winking at Mads. 'She's

a strong girl, I'm not sure how long I'll be able to fight her off.'

When she came back downstairs Lyndsey found them both sitting at the kitchen table with a pot of tea and a plate full of toasted teacakes. It felt strange to sit chatting about nothing in particular, like an oasis of normality in the maelstrom of her life, but after a couple of minutes she relaxed and joined in. When she glanced up at the clock she was surprised to see it was almost four o'clock.

'We'd best be going, Mads.'

'OK, let me visit the little girls' room and I'll be with you.'

She grabbed her bag and went upstairs.

'Are you sure you're fine?' asked Bert.

'Yes, of course. Everything will sort itself out.'

'Well, anything you need or want to ask, don't forget I'm here.'

'I won't. Stop fussing, Grandad. Can you see why I didn't want to bother you?'

'I only worry when you're keeping things from me. You don't have to, I'm on your side.'

Lyndsey leaned over and gave him a kiss on the cheek as she stood.

'I'm very grateful for it, but we need to get going. I'll be home later.'

She went upstairs to grab a jacket then checked the timetables on her phone while Mads said her goodbyes to Bert. Before long they were out the door and on the H91 bus to Hounslow.

'You sure we're not going to be too early?' asked Mads.

'No, it's Sunday afternoon. They'll be watching the football.'

'Who's playing?'

'I'm not sure it matters. Beer, football and pool was a regular Sunday ritual for them all.'

'I wouldn't mind a game of pool. Did you see my snooker table at home?'

'I did, very impressive. How did you get it up to the second floor?'

'We didn't. The previous owners left it behind. I imagine the cost of moving it outweighed the value of the table. We had the table re-clothed and balanced, I only wish more people came round to play.'

The Polar was busy when they arrived. Most people's attention was focused on the televisions positioned at either end of the bar. A small group of men congregated by a pool table.

'Is that them?'

'No, Barry's mates will be in the back where the big screen is. Let's get a drink here and walk through.'

They walked the short distance across the dark wooden floorboards to the bar where Mads ordered them both a pint of Abbot. They carried them through a double width doorway to a back room three times the size of the front bar, that doubled up as a restaurant. The smell of curry and spices gave a clue as to the majority of the available menu.

A huge television was prominent on the far wall, facing them as they entered. The noise the football crowd and commentator was piped through the bar's sound system. Lyndsey nudged Mads and nodded at a pool table just to their left. She leant in to Mads' ear.

'Paul was Barry's best mate. He's the one on the table now. If anybody has any information, he will be the one to ask.'

He potted the black ball and they walked across to him.

'Hi, Paul,' she said, raising her voice so as to be heard above the cacophony.

He turned towards them.

'Hello Lyndsey. Unusual for you to come down here. Barry's not here, love.'

'Yes, we came to see you.'

There were a couple of catcalls from the group behind him.

'Why's that?'

'We are interested in what Barry did on Thursday nights,' said Mads.

There was a brief pause. 'He always comes down here with us. Boys' night out, you know that, Lynds.'

'But he hasn't been here for a few weeks, has he?'

'What do you mean? Where else would he go? He wouldn't miss Thursday night, would he lads?'

A few of his mates shook their heads in agreement.

'I'll tell you what,' said Mads. 'I'll play you pool for it.'

More catcalls came from the crowd, a little louder this time.

'Shut up you lot. Play me pool for what?'

'If you win I'll give you £20. If I beat you, you'll buy us both a pint and answer our questions.'

'Nah, that's stupid. I'm telling you the truth. Save your money.'

His mates started laughing and taunting him.

'You scared of playing a girl, Paul?' shouted one.

He glared back at them. 'No, course not, but she can put her name up and wait like everyone else. It's only fair, innit?'

'Here you go, love. I'm on next. You can take my spot,' said one of his friends. He walked over to a blackboard on the wall, rubbed his name out and wrote BLONDIE in its place and added his name to the bottom of the list. 'Unless Paul's too much of a pussy to play you, of course.'

That comment elicited a roar of laughter from the crowd. Mads took advantage of the moment.

'So what do you say, Paul? You don't want your mates to think you're a coward, do you?'

He shrugged, his face reddening with embarrassment. 'Fine, it's your funeral.'

Lyndsey walked across to an empty, tall table and

stood there with a smile on her face. She'd seen Mads play pool before, and with the snooker table in her house she knew she would have kept her eye in over the last couple of years. Ten minutes later, Paul was making his way across to the bar, shoulders hunched, pretending he was unaware of the sarcastic shouts from his mates. Mads walked across to Lyndsey and indicated towards the other bar with her head. They went back through to the relative quiet and sat at an oval table in an alcove while they waited for Paul.

'Why do they think they have a god given right to beat us at games?' said Mads.

'I think it's to increase the fun factor for us when they don't. Aren't you staying on the table?'

'No, I made my point. There's no guarantee he'll tell us the truth, of course, but as it's illegal to torture him and I'm not going to sleep with him, it's all I'm prepared to do.'

'Oh I don't know. He's so embarrassed at losing to you at pool, I can't imagine he'd want to admit that you overpowered and tortured him.'

'Fair point, we'll leave torture on the table as a last resort. Let's hope we don't need to, though. Neither of us have a dungeon and all the best torturing takes place in dungeons.'

'We could get him to dig you one.'

'He's a bit out of shape for that. We're not trying to

kill him.'

'It's only beer blubber. He'll soon toughen up.'

'Well, if you're sure. Tell you what, I'll employ you as works manager.'

They laughed and Mads looked around the room. It had a strange décor, as if it didn't know what it wanted to be. There was a fan over the pool table lights and mock oil lamps above the bar. The ceiling was painted white, accentuating the fake beams stuck to it. The wallpaper was a deep claret with gold plants of some kind that resembled a cross between a thistle and a leafy cauliflower. The wallpaper wouldn't look out of place in an Indian restaurant, and Mads thought it ironic that while the same wallpaper also adorned the walls in the restaurant bar, it had been painted light cream there.

'What plant is that on the wallpaper?'

Lyndsey looked at it for a few moments.

'Beats me, Is it a cardoon or an artichoke thistle?'

'I've no idea. It's strange, is what it is.'

She continued casting her eyes around. A selection of old hunting prints were on the walls and the stained pub windows looked as if they might be originals that had survived modern attempts at renovation. Between the double doorway they had walked through and another door leading to the same bar, hung a small jukebox unit. Past the small door, in the corner was an old oak dresser and a suggestions box. A few more mock oil lamps were on the walls, looking even more out of place with the stark modernity of the television screens.

Paul made his way to the table carrying three pints of beer.

'Here you go,' he said putting them on the table. 'Where did you learn to play pool like that?'

Mads smiled at him. 'I come from a sizeable family and things could get competitive, particularly with my brothers. If you fancy your chances at wrestling, just say the word.'

Paul stayed quiet, but she relished the look of uncertainty in his eyes.

'So tell us, where did Barry go on Thursday nights?'

His eyes darted towards Lyndsey.

'Don't worry,' she said. 'You won't be getting him into any trouble.'

'So why don't you ask him?'

'You first,' said Mads.

Paul stared her in the eye then at the table. After a moment he shrugged.

'I don't suppose it matters. Two or three months ago we were all sitting outside and got talking to a couple of east Europeans. They told us about a regular poker game in Brentford so Barry's been going there on Thursdays.'

'He's been playing poker?' The news struck Mads as an anti-climax.

'As far as I know. Poker's not my game. I'd always rather pool.' He grimaced at Mads. 'Until today.'

'Did he win?'

'First couple of weeks he was full of himself and tried to persuade me to go along too, but I figured he'd got the message since. I guess he might also have started losing.'

His eyes flitted between the women.

'There's nothing else, honest. Check with him if you don't believe me.'

Lyndsey smiled. 'So what about the rest of the week?'

A panicked expression crossed his face.

'I don't know, Lynds. I only come down on Thursday on weekdays. You'll need to ask him.'

'That could be tricky,' said Mads.

He raised his eyebrows at her. 'Why, where's he gone?'

She glanced at Lyndsey who indicated to her to continue.

'Someone killed him yesterday morning.'

He slumped back in his chair.

'You're kidding? Who? How? Where? I don't know where to start.' He picked up his pint and took a long drink.

'He was stabbed at the market,' said Lyndsey. 'As for who, we're trying to find that out before the police arrest me.'

'Shit, I had no idea. You must be beside yourself.'

She shrugged. 'I've had better weekends. So where was this poker game?'

'I don't know. Hang on.' He darted towards the doorway to the back bar and beckoned to someone before returning to the table. One of his friends who also had close cropped hair and a green Harrington strolled across.

'What do you want?'

'Andy, where was the card game those blokes were on about the other week.'

'Brentford, but I don't know where. Ask Barry.'

'Didn't they give you a number though?'

He rummaged through his jacket pockets before producing a crumpled scrap of paper.

'Here you go. Keep it, I'm not going to bother.'

'Cheers,' said Paul, turning back towards the table. 'Here you go, this is one of the guys we were talking to. Tibor.'

'Great, thanks, but if you think of anything can you give me a call,' said Mads handing him her name and number.

'Yes, of course. I'll ask around, maybe the others will

come up with some ideas, too.'

Paul walked back to the pool table with Andy leaving the women on their own.

'So what now?' asked Mads before taking a drink. 'Can you play poker?'

Lyndsey thought for a moment. 'I wouldn't know where to start. I have an idea, though,' she said before pulling a card from her pocket along with her phone. She dialled the number on it.

'Hello?'

'John, Lyndsey from yesterday.'

'Still stalking me, huh? What can I do for you?'

She laughed. 'Can you play poker?'

He paused for a few moments. 'Yes, but only Hold'Em and Omaha. Why, what do you need?'

She gave Mads a thumbs up. 'That should be good enough. Do you want to meet for a drink and we'll fill you in on the details?'

'Sounds good. I'm in Brentford today, so how about The Phoenix?'

'That will work for us, would seven be OK?'

'Perfect, I'll see you both there.'

She put her phone away and smiled at Mads.

'We have ourselves a poker player. Let's finish these drinks, grab something to eat somewhere and get to

Brentford.'

They arrived at The Phoenix ten minutes early. It was a typical old Victorian style pub, with lots of dark wood and character. A few men, who Lyndsey imagined were the remains of the football crowd, were perched on stools chatting around the bar. Most of the tables were occupied too, but no one was playing darts so they sat at a table in a corner close to the dart board. A Golden Labrador plodded his way across to them and sniffed the air, hoping they had food. Having satisfied himself that there was none, he trudged his way back again in search of more dog-friendly customers.

'That's strange,' said Mads nodding towards the back corner of the bar.

A big screen TV was mounted high on the wall showing cycling, but below it a bench seat and table created a cosy little nook. Lyndsey glanced over and saw Martin and Mary both huddled together.

'What about it?'

'Mary denied there was anything between them.'

'You never know, maybe he made a move.'

Mads shrugged. 'Perhaps, though she was thoroughly uninterested. Happy for him to be running around after her like a lapdog with the van and everything but nothing more. That was the impression I got.'

'Your questioning could have awakened something inside that she was unaware of. Why were you asking stuff like that?'

'I like to get a bit of background. It breaks the ice and gets people chatting. Did you expect me to be opening with "OK, Bugsy, why did you kill Barry?"'

'Haha, no, of course not. I didn't give it much thought. Maybe, and I'm only putting this out there as a remote possibility, but maybe she didn't want a reporter outing her private life in the local paper.'

'Fair enough, you might have a point.'

John walked in and Lyndsey waved to attract his attention.

'Hi, you two OK for drinks?'

'We're good,' said Lyndsey, 'and we got you a London Pride.' She pushed the beer across the table.

'Thanks,' he said pulling out a stool and sitting down. 'So what's this about poker?'

'We've found out Barry was involved in a game every week. Neither of us can play, so we wondered if you could check it out for us. We'll stake you.'

'Fair enough. Where is it?'

'Somewhere in Brentford. Here's the number.' She passed over the piece of paper. 'Tell Tibor you met him a few weeks ago at the Polar in Hounslow. I don't expect he'll remember who he gave his number to.'

'Will do. Back in a minute, I'll phone from outside the door where the TV isn't blaring in my lughole.'

Five minutes later he was back.

'All set up for tomorrow about eight. £500 buy-in, is that OK?'

Mads nodded. 'No problem. I'll withdraw the cash from the bank. Where will we meet you?'

'We're looking at the far end of the High Street, so what about The Pye around seven?'

'Fine by me, you Lynds?'

'Yes, of course. You'll be picking me up in the morning, won't you? We are going to visit Bill and Rhonda's shop.'

'I wouldn't miss it. This is exciting. I'm beginning to feel like a real private eye.'

26

Mads ran out to the car next morning at ten, trying to stay as dry as possible. It was a miserable day, dark grey clouds in every direction and rain that was predicted to be teeming until mid-afternoon.

'I knew I'd need a trilby and a dirty old raincoat,' she muttered as she slammed the car door shut.

When she got to Lyndsey's, she phoned to tell her she was outside and waited in the car. A few minutes later, Lyndsey wrenched open the door and dived into the passenger seat.

'What a glorious day. Glad the weather wasn't like this over the weekend.'

'You'd still be drying out. You don't have a tent like Mary, do you?'

'No, there are a couple of clear plastic sheets in the van to cover the merchandise, but nothing for the poor mug who stands there trying to sell everything. Do you know where we're going?'

'Yes, you gave me the address last night. Shouldn't take too long to get to Richmond.'

She typed the post code into the satnav and they were soon on their way, the dulcet tones of Homer Simpson directing them. With the weather, everyone and their dogs had taken to their cars, but after forty minutes of pulsating nose to tail action they arrived at the antique shop.

'Woohoo! You have reached your destination,' shouted Homer.

'Thanks, I don't suppose you can tell me where to find a parking spot, could you?' asked Mads.

If he did, Homer was keeping the information to himself, so she followed the signs to the car park near the railway station.

'Sorry, we might get a bit wet.'

'I'm sure we'll survive,' said Lyndsey, producing a small umbrella from her coat pocket.

'Ever the practical one,' said Mads. 'I gave up with umbrellas as I always left them somewhere. I felt I was supplying half of London with freebies.'

'Well, don't tell, but I found this one on a train.'

'In that case, there's every chance it's one of mine. And you're welcome.'

They both laughed and started walking. They took about ten minutes to wend their way past countless grumpy looking people before they reached the shop. They huddled in the doorway while Lyndsey shook as much of the rain from the umbrella as she could before closing it. Mads pushed the door open and the tinkling of a small brass bell hanging on the inside announced their arrival.

'Ooh, I can't be trusted in places like this. I should give you my credit card to hold in case I go crazy,' she whispered to Lyndsey as she closed the door behind them.

'Yes, they don't bring their best stuff to market. Some of these items are gorgeous, though they also have price tags to match.'

A plump, middle-aged woman wearing a Laura Ashley floral dress appeared from the back of the shop.

'Good morning, what a ghastly day. May I help you with something, or are you just browsing?'

Lyndsey poked her head around Mads who had obscured her from view.

'Hi Rhonda. How are you both after Saturday's excitement?'

'Hello love. Sorry, I didn't see you behind your friend. We were a bit shaken, but I think we're over the worst. How are you, though? Wasn't Barry your boyfriend?'

'We'd broken up, but it still came as a shock. We're

here because the police have me high on their suspect list so we are doing some investigating of our own.'

Rhonda's RP pronunciation fell away revealing the lilting Welsh accent of her childhood.

'Oh for goodness sakes. It's ridiculous to think you had anything to do with killing him. Come through to the office, the two of you, and I'll make a cup of tea.'

'Thanks, that would be lovely,' she said as she walked past Mads, who reluctantly stopped cooing over half the items in the shop and followed.

They both sat on a pair of wooden chairs Rhonda directed them to before she went through a door they assumed led to the kitchen. The office was small and a desk was in the corner with a computer on it and a couple more chairs, one in front and one at the end. A filing cabinet stood behind the door they had come through, next to a small oil heater.

'This is cosy,' said Lyndsey when Rhonda reappeared carrying a tray containing a volumous teapot, a jug, a bowl and four mugs.

'Yes, we don't often entertain guests but it serves the purpose. Bill will be through in a moment or two, he's rummaging around in the storeroom out back.'

'You have a storeroom? These shops are so small and quaint I didn't think there was much more space than could be seen when you walk in?' asked Lyndsey.

'Well, most would say we have a sizeable shed in the back yard, but that's what we use it as. The police still have all our furniture from the market so Bill's taking the opportunity to tidy up. With any luck, he may find some old trinkets we forgot we had.'

Almost as if he knew he was going to be mentioned, Bill walked into the office and sat his rotund bulk into the computer chair.

'Not so much old trinkets as rubbish we should have thrown away ages ago,' he said. 'The dustmen will be cursing us tomorrow. So Lyndsey, to what do we owe this pleasure?'

Lyndsey introduced everyone and they smiled and nodded at each other.

'We came to ask if you could remember anything unusual from Saturday. The police think I killed Barry, so we're conducting our own unofficial investigation.'

'You're kidding me, right?' said Bill with a hearty laugh. 'How do they imagine you could have done that?'

' From what I can gather, with the aid of an unknown accomplice who did the heavy lifting. From where I'm sitting, you need to want to believe it for the concept to make any sense.'

'That's an understatement.' He looked across at

Rhonda who shrugged and stood to pour the tea.

'I said the same,' she replied. 'How do you take yours?'

'Black, no sugar,' said Lyndsey.

'Same for me, please,' said Mads.

Rhonda poured all four of them a mugful and sat down again.

'There you go, loves. Help yourselves. Do you want a drop of cold water to cool it down a tad?'

They shook their heads.

'Well, we've both been over Saturday's events with the police what feels like a thousand times,' said Bill. 'We couldn't come up with anything out of the ordinary, could we pet?'

'No, but the wardrobe was near the far end of our stall. You'll remember how we unload, Lyndsey. We drive along, taking everything out a few pieces at a time to save carrying them any farther than we need to. We must have been unsighted, or in the back of the van.'

'Yes, I don't imagine you witnessed the murder, but anything or anyone unusual? You have a perfect view of the alcove from your stall, so you might have spotted something everyone else missed.'

'Oh, I see,' she said picking up her mug and taking a sip. 'Let me think. We were first to arrive, as usual. About 4.30, right, Bill?'

'Yes, Bob and Jools showed up around five, so we chatted to them for a few minutes.'

'That's right, Martin and Mary were along soon after because they'd just finished putting her cover up when you got there.'

'Yes, I remember they were laying stuff out when I got there.'

'Let me think, now,' Rhonda continued. 'Ranjit and Sammy were setting up, so they must have arrived a little after us. Barry showed up late, but that was nothing out of the ordinary. Didn't he come across to speak to you once he was set up and his music was playing?'

'Yes, he did,' confirmed Lyndsey. 'That was right on opening time because the dubious pleasure of his company was cut short by him getting a customer.'

'Yes,' said Rhonda. 'Big chap with a limp.'

'His name's John. We've spoken to him and are sure he had nothing to do with it.'

'Shame, they were having a spirited argument. He would make an ideal suspect. I pointed them out to you, didn't I Bill?'

'Yes, but he walked away while Barry was still alive.'

'Oh, I didn't know. Why didn't you tell me?'

'I know this will come as a shock, dear, but I don't tell you everything I see on a daily basis.'

She glared at him out of the corner of her eye, before turning her attention back to Lyndsey.

'While they were arguing, you went to the catering truck.'

She nodded, amazed at Rhonda's recall abilities. 'Yes, John and Barry had disappeared by the time I got back.'

'After that, I saw Martin duck under his flap to go to get some food. At least that's where I thought he went. Did you run into him while you were there?'

'No, I didn't, but that doesn't mean much. Maybe he joined the queue while I was waiting to be served. Madge made my breakfast to order so it took longer than most.'

'Those are all the comings and goings I can think of before you got back. It was a slow morning. You had someone browsing. There were a couple interested in mirrors and their daughter who was looking at Mary's paintings. Aside from that, you were talking to a man just as the customer who found the body and her friend screamed when they opened the wardrobe. Well, I say customer. I doubt she will be now.'

Lyndsey glanced at Mads who was scribbling in her notepad.

'Wow, as comprehensive a breakdown as we could wish for. If you do think of anything else, anything at all, could you give me a call, please?' asked Mads, handing over

another scrap of paper with her name and number on. 'Or Lynds, but I've been giving everyone this one so it makes sense to give it to you as well.'

'Yes, of course.'

'We are frustrated we didn't see who put Barry into the wardrobe,' said Bill. 'That could have sewn everything up if we had.'

'Not to worry. How are you both? It's been ages since we last spoke,' asked Lyndsey.

They all chatted whilst drinking their tea. An hour later the bell on the front door jangled again.

'Oh, what are we like?' said Lyndsey. 'Keeping you from working. We'd better get going and leave you to it.'

'It's been lovely catching up,' said Rhonda, 'and meeting you, Mads. I'm sure we'll be seeing you again sometime.'

'I hope so, and maybe next time I can relieve you of a few of the items in the shop,' she said as she got up.

Bill jolted the desk as he stood to shake goodbye, waking the PC up from its sleep and displaying a wallpaper of him, Rhonda and someone else Mads recognised. She stared at the screen, transfixed for a moment before shaking Bill's hand, then Rhonda's.

'Is that your daughter?' she asked.

'Yes,' said Rhonda.

'She's very pretty.'

'Thanks. If I hadn't been at the birth I'd question whether she was mine,' she said, laughing.

Mads and Lyndsey turned and went through the door towards the shop. As they walked through, they saw Inspector Savage standing there waiting.

'Well, well, strange seeing the two of you here.'

'We thought we'd pop in and check that Bill and Rhonda were OK,' said Lyndsey, using her best sweet and innocent voice.

'Is that so? Not meddling I hope, because if you're hankering to try your luck as private eyes I feel I should lock you both up for your own good.'

'Nothing of the sort had occurred to us, had it Mads?'

Mads shook her head and smiled at him.

'Well, make sure it doesn't,' said the inspector, moving aside to let them pass.

They left without another word, pausing in the doorway to put the umbrella up again before heading towards the station.

'Do you want to grab a coffee?' asked Lyndsey. 'It will give us a chance to go through everything while we wait for the rain to stop.'

'Yes, sure,' said Mads distractedly. 'That might be a good idea.'

They found a small independent café along one of the alleyways between the High Street and Richmond Green and both ordered black coffee. They were the only customers and they took their drinks to a table in the corner by the window where they could talk without being overheard. Mads took out her notepad and glanced over her notes.

'Why, whenever someone remembers a new person in this timeline, are they talking to you?'

'Sorry, what?'

'Rhonda said you had a customer right before the body was discovered.'

Lyndsey looked sheepish for a moment. 'Oh him, he had nothing to do with Barry.'

'How do you know?'

'He gave me some photos.'

'What photos?'

'Forget it, they're nothing to do with the murder.'

Mads stared across the table at her for a few seconds before looking back down at the notepad. A man entered the cafe looking drenched and made his way to the service counter.

'You know almost everything from the notes I took at the market. The only person to pay attention to anything Saturday morning is Rhonda, the rest are all making like wise monkeys. But, and here's where things become interesting, I chatted with a couple of girls in the café yesterday morning after you left to set up.'

'What girls?'

'They work at the supermarket down the road. The interesting part is that they knew Barry's other ex-girl-friend, Sharon, as she worked there too.'

'Right,' said Lyndsey through gritted teeth.

The man placed his coffee of the table behind theirs and, having removed his coat and hung it on a chair, sat with his back to Lyndsey. Mads leaned across the table and lowered her voice a little.

'Well, when I disappeared yesterday, I met her for lunch. She knew nothing about you - still doesn't - and didn't even know he was dead. She came across as genuine, so I don't think she killed him, though to say she wasn't upset would be an understatement.'

'Bad break up?'

'You could say that. He dumped her when she fell pregnant and she tried to kill herself. She got out of hospital a couple of weeks ago.'

Lyndsey sat back and raised her hands to cover her gaping mouth.

'You're kidding me? You're making it difficult for me to hate this woman.'

'Like I say, I'm certain she had nothing to do with his murder, but that doesn't mean someone close to her didn't.'

'Like who?'

'That's why I stared at the computer wallpaper in Bill and Rhonda's office. Sharon is their daughter.'

'Bill and Rhonda? The Sharon you're talking about is their daughter? But she's little more than a kid.'

'Think about it. Either of them could take the knife without attracting much attention, the body was found on their pitch, and they have a strong motive now we can connect them with Sharon.'

'But, still.'

'And isn't it a little strange Rhonda remembers everything that happened that morning except the most important detail?'

'I'm not sure we can read too much into that. When she retires she'll be the old lady on her street sat behind a twitching curtain. I must admit though, her powers of recall were a little spooky.'

'Or rehearsed?'

Lyndsey thought for a moment. 'If she's had to go

through it numerous times with the police, that might account for the exceptional memory?'

'Fair point. I'm not sure how we'd prove it, even if it was them. In a cosy mystery novel we'd go back to accuse them, they'd panic and tie us up somewhere where we'd be rescued by the hunky detective just as they were about to kill and dispose of us.'

Lyndsey raised her eyebrows. 'If it's all the same to you, I'd rather not do that. Not only is Savage more chunk than hunk, I lack faith in his sense of drama and timing.'

'I know what you mean. What were they wearing Saturday, do you remember?'

'Let me think. Rhonda had on a dark brown jumper and a pair of beige slacks. Bill wore a black puffa jacket and grey trousers. Why?'

'Was that before or after the body was found?'

'After, because everyone was standing around talking. I didn't pay much attention before.'

'No bloodstains or anything?'

'I think both me and the police might have spotted that.'

'Yes, I suppose so. What if someone did it for them?'

'Who? They don't come across to me as people who would move in the same circles as a hitman, and even if they did, they'd employ someone with more sense than to leave the body in their wardrobe. Or should I say my wardrobe. It's just sunk in that it was mine. Barry took it there to sell.'

'It was yours? The links between you and his death keep piling up, don't they? Do Bill and Rhonda have any other children?'

'Only Sharon. I remember her from years ago when she was so high,' said Lyndsey indicating a little taller than the table. 'Ugh, I still can't believe her and Barry.'

'If not them we're back to square one. I'm still placing them at the top of our suspect list.'

'I can't help feeling we're missing something. Does it make any sense that nobody saw anything?'

'No, even if it was someone from outside. I'm sure no one was entirely truthful, though that doesn't mean they lied about anything relevant. Just market stuff, like Ranjit implying his stock is pure silk when it's art silk.'

'But nothing about Barry.'

'Not that I noticed, but as you say it makes no sense that no one saw a thing. Even if they had seen something and kept quiet, though, it still wouldn't mean they're guilty. They might be scared or not want to get involved.'

'I suppose so. With any luck the poker game will give us more options.'

'Glad you mentioned that, remind me to get the

money out when we leave.' Mads looked through the window at the pouring rain. 'Shall we eat and give it another chance to stop raining?'

At half past one the torrent eased off to a light drizzle and they left the café to head for the car.

As the café door clicked shut, the man plucked a phone from his pocket and made a call.

'Yes?'

'I think he might be telling the truth. They've not mentioned the photos all the time they've been in earshot.'

'So what have they done?'

'Very little, they went to an antique shop this morning, since then they've sat in a café. The only thing they've talked about is that kid who was stabbed at the market on Saturday. Now the rain's let up, they're on their way to Lyndsey's place. Do you want me to stick with them?'

There was a pause.

'No, come back here. There are things that need doing, and if the police are sniffing about we need to keep our distance. I have other ways to keep tabs on Lyndsey Marshall.'

When they got back to Lyndsey's the rain had stopped.
Mads followed her upstairs to her room and sat on the bed.

'Could I see those photos?'

'They're nothing to do with this. Forget I mentioned
them.'

'Sorry, doll. You hired me to solve the case and until I
do, everything's my business. Understand?'

Lyndsey couldn't help but laugh at Mads' mock noir
accent.

'If I do will you leave it alone?'

'Of course,' said Mads, crossing her fingers behind her
back.

Lyndsey took the box out of the drawer and sat down
again before handing it over.

'They're just pictures of my parents,' she said.

Mads opened the lid and started flicking through.

'They're older than I expected,' she said. 'When did they die? Ten years ago?'

'Fifteen. I thought that, but figured my memory was playing tricks on me. Do you want some tea?'

'Love some, please.'

She carried on searching while Lyndsey went downstairs to the kitchen. There was something wrong with these pictures. If Lyndsey's parents had died fifteen years ago, judging by how they looked in the photos they must have been in their fifties when Lyndsey was born. And why wasn't she in them? They would have taken her on a family holiday, and it didn't look like much business was being done.

Mads started studying them closer, hunting for anything that might give her a clue as to the location or the rough date. The weather was good, and from the looks of the architecture and other people in the photos she guessed at Southern Europe or South America. Possibly even Asia. She cursed herself for not having travelled more.

Add that to the ever growing list of things to do now your inner Mads has reawakened.

One photo caught her eye and she pulled it out of the box for closer inspection. Lyndsey's parents were outside a shop and she was hoping that something in the window might give a clue to their whereabouts. A poster or sign maybe. Anything that contained a recognisable language. She angled the picture towards the light and almost rested her nose on it to get as good a look as she could. As she studied the photo, she caught her breath.

No, that can't be right. That makes no sense.

30

Hearing Lyndsey on the stairs, Mads put the photo into her pocket and carried on flicking through the others. She came in the room, placed a couple of mugs of tea on the bedside table and tossed a packet of Bourbons onto the bed.

'Here you go, help yourself,' she said. 'I told you the photos had nothing to do with Barry.'

'They're nice, though. Where were they taken?'

'It's odd, I have no idea. It must have been one of those weeks when I found myself enjoying an impromptu holiday with Grandad while they disappeared on business.'

'And someone just gave them to you, Saturday?'

Lyndsey opened the biscuits and grabbed a couple. 'Yes, right before Barry's body was discovered. It's been a strange weekend all round. Someone came up to the stall yesterday hoping to find some photographs that a friend of his had had stolen. Weird guy, had a stare that could pierce rock.'

'Did you tell him about these?'

'No, what would he want with pictures of Mum and Dad? He must have been looking for a different set. I told him, aside from the old postcards we don't stock anything like that. He asked me to give him a call if I was offered any and went away.'

'So he gave you his number?'

'Yes, he wrote it down for me. Why, what's the big deal?'

'Nothing, I'm just curious. It's a strange coincidence for photos to come up twice over the weekend when you don't sell them. Did you do a reverse directory enquiry on him?'

Lyndsey laughed. 'Mads, you're scaring me. I know you're like a dog with a bone when you think you're onto something, but this is no more than a distraction. We need to focus on Barry.'

'Yes, you're right. Sorry.'

She replaced the lid and handed the box back. Lyndsey returned it to the drawer.

'You knew him better than I did, Lynds. What do you suggest we do now? Where can we dig up some dirt on him?'

'We have five hours or so until we arranged to meet John. I can think of one place where we might find something.' She pulled a keyring from her pocket and jangled it in front of her. 'Guess who has the keys to his flat.'

Mads' opened her eyes wide. 'We couldn't. Could we? If we got caught it would be breaking and entering.'

'Not really. With these, it would only be entering.'

'Let's hope no one catches us because I'm not sure that technicality will add up to a mountain of marbles in court.'

Lyndsey walked across to a dressing table and opened the drawer. She pulled out two pairs of gloves.

'We don't want to leave fingerprints all over the place.'

'Good thinking, Raffles.'

She took a watch and a necklace from a jewellery box.

'And just in case we stumble into anyone. I went back to look for these.'

Lyndsey picked up her coat and put them in the pocket followed by some gloves. She threw the other pair across to Mads.

'You've done this before,' said Mads with a smile on her face. 'Give me a couple of minutes to freshen up in the bathroom and I'll be with you.'

31

Mads locked the bathroom door, put the toilet cover down and sat on it. She pulled the photo from her pocket and stared at it again. There was no mistake. This was huge. Worse still, she couldn't tell Lyndsey, it would tear her apart. Not that there would ever be a good time, but first things first. Solve the murder, then think of a way to tell her.

That was the sensible thing to do.

But what if everything was linked? Just, what if?

She looked at the photo again. The shop; the window; the clock displaying the time and date. Assuming it was correct, and there was no reason Mads could think of that it wouldn't be, these pictures were three months old. And Lyndsey's parents—if it was them—were looking rather more bright-eyed and bushy-tailed than was expected of people who had been dead fifteen years.

After dropping the car at Mads' house they caught the 237 to Hounslow. After a short walk, Lyndsey led Mads up a garden path towards a semi-detached house. At the front door, she rang the bottom bell and waited.

'Who do you think is going to answer?'

'It's worth checking, just in case. We don't want to go blundering in and find the forensics unit turning the place over.'

Lyndsey took out her keys and opened the front door. Inside was a short hallway with a door to their left and a flight of stairs leading up. The door had two strips of police tape across it in an X shape.

'Now what?' asked Mads.

'We've come this far,' said Lyndsey unlocking the flat door and pushing it open.

Mads grabbed her arm. 'What are you doing? I don't

want to get arrested.'

Lyndsey put her gloves on. 'You can wait outside if you like. Call and warn me if anyone shows up.'

Mads thought for a moment before taking the gloves from her pocket. 'No, let's stick together.'

They ducked under the tape and closed the door behind them. A computer was in the corner facing them, next to a flat screen TV and a stereo system. The speakers were on brackets aiming towards an old, threadbare sofa, behind the door. A coffee table sat in front of it and CDs were stacked on shelves attached to the wall to their right between two more doorways.

'This is spartan,' whispered Mads, flicking through a small pile of opened post.

'Yes, he kept his merchandise in a lockup along with a collection of magazines that he assured me was far too valuable to recycle. Why are we whispering?'

'I don't want upstairs to hear us and phone the police.'

'Fair point. Back in a moment, I'll dig around in the bedroom.'

Lyndsey disappeared through the left hand doorway. Mads finished reading the mail and went through the right hand door to the kitchen. The sink was full of dirty plates and dishes piled up as if they were expected to wash themselves. She searched through the drawers and cupboards and poked her head into the bathroom at the back before heading for the bedroom.

'Turned up anything in here?' she asked.

Lyndsey closed the drawer she had been rifling through and opened the wardrobe.

'Found his little black book.'

'Brilliant, we can call the inaugural meeting of the Barry exes club. Will Shepherds Bush Empire do, or will we need a bigger venue?'

Lyndsey shot her a glare. 'More to the point, it contains all his passwords and key codes. Was there anything of interest in the mail?'

'How much rent did you pay for this place?'

'£700 a month. I gave Barry my share and he paid the landlord because the flat was in his name.'

'According to a threatening letter, it's at least two months outstanding.'

Lyndsey rummaged through the wardrobe then closed the door.

'I'm pleased the flat's in his name. At last, a small glint of light at the end of the tunnel. Come on, let's check his computer then get out of here.'

They went through to the front room and she turned on the PC.

'Let's hope he didn't change the login.'

When the desktop appeared. She pulled a USB stick from her pocket and plugged it in.

'Right, what do we want? Documents and photos first, I think.'

She opened a directory window and dragged the folders to the stick. While they copied she scanned the desktop but couldn't see anything interesting.

'Anything else you can think of?'

'Open the C: drive and search for anything suspicious.'

Lyndsey opened it but nothing unusual leapt out at her.

'Try the accounts folder.'

'Why? We know he owes money all over the place.'

'Yes, but an accounts folder is the least likely place a girlfriend will look to find anything she isn't supposed to.'

'You're sneakier than I give you credit for,' she said, opening the folder. Below a few spreadsheets titled by year was a file named zzzz.zip. She clicked the back button and dragged the whole folder over to the drive.

'May as well take the lot. Anything else you can think of?'

'Maybe delete the zip file when you've done? There might be things in there you wouldn't want to be made public. Apart from that, no. Let's finish up and run.'

'OK, was there anything in the kitchen?'

'Yes, you need to do the washing up, but it'll wait.'

'That figures. I'm afraid the landlord can do that for him.'

The files finished copying and she ejected the drive before yanking it out, deleting the file from the computer and clicking Shutdown.

'Yes, because we wouldn't want to risk turning it off at the switch.' said Mads.

'Force of habit. Let me check the sofa then we can go.'

She hunted beneath the seat cushions but found nothing.

'I think we're done.'

They went out, ducking under the police tape once more, and closed the door behind them. As they turned towards the front door, the grating of a key being inserted into the lock echoed through the hallway.

'Quick,' she hissed, grabbing Mads by the arm and dragging her beneath the stairs where an old bicycle was stored. They both squatted down, holding their breath. Someone entered and slammed the door shut behind them. Next they heard the sound of keys clinking together and Barry's door being unlocked. Lyndsey peered around the stairs just in time to see Inspector Savage disappearing into the flat and closing the door behind him.

She waited a few seconds then turned her head. 'Let's make ourselves scarce.'

They crept to the door and opened it, closing it from outside using the key so as not to attract attention by slamming it, and scurried up the garden path. Mads breathed a huge sigh of relief as they turned out of the gate.

'That was close. Who was it?'

'Inspector Savage. Let's hope he didn't see us through the window as we ran out.'

'You do know you'll have my mother to answer to if you get me arrested and that's not something I'd wish on anyone.'

'We were lucky. A couple of moments either way and he'd have caught us red handed.'

Lyndsey took her gloves off and slid her hand into her pocket. 'Oh no!' she said, stopping dead in her tracks.

'What's up?'

'My watch, it's not here.'

Mads raised her hand to her mouth. 'You're kidding? You dropped it in the flat?'

'I think so. I had it when I put my gloves on because I checked I didn't pull it out with them.'

'Was it expensive?'

'I wouldn't think so, it was a present from Barry.'

'So just sentimental value?'

'Not even, I'd rather forget he existed.'

'So what's the problem?'

'The watch was personalised. He had my name engraved on the back.'

33

They stared at each other for a few seconds.

'So what shall we do? Wait until he leaves?'

'I could knock on the door now and pretend I came by to find it.'

Mads raised an eyebrow. 'Don't you think that might be suspicious? We only ran into him this morning. It would be strange you appear at the door just as he's in the flat.'

'Yes, you're right. Best make ourselves scarce. I can always say I left it behind when I moved out.'

'If you're sure. What shall we do now?'

'While we're here, we might as well go and check his lockup space.'

'Is it close by?'

'Yes, not far. He wrote his access codes in the book so we should be able to walk straight in.'

As Lyndsey predicted, they typed the entry code

and entered the storage warehouse without a problem. It was huge, like an aircraft hangar with various sized metal rooms arranged into rows, rather like a locker room would be in a gym for giants. The corridor in front of them was as wide as a single lane road. Lyndsey veered right and pressed the button to call the lift which they rode to the second floor. When the doors opened again, they walked out and turned left.

'What are we looking for?' asked Mads.

'Number 2136. If we follow this to the end and turn right, it should be along the third turning, assuming he hasn't changed rooms since I last came here.'

'How have you managed to remember the room?'

'I don't, he wrote it in the book like a phone number. The last four digits will be the code to open the padlock.'

'Sneaky, how did you work that out?'

Lyndsey flicked through and pointed at an entry.

'I'm in here, LB 812Ø 1987. That gave me one of my first clues.'

'Was that your number at the newspaper?'

'Mads, I'm hurt that you don't remember my birthday,' she said with a raised eyebrow.

'Oh no, Bob and me over the same weekend. How will you cope?'

'It will be a struggle, I can't deny it, but I'm sure I'll

survive.'

They both laughed.

'No, but carry on. Barry's magic book?'

'He had a memory like a sieve for anything like that. I figured it was likely some of the other entries weren't exactly what they seemed. That way if he lost it anyone who found it wouldn't suspect it was anything other than a contact book. The noughts with lines through are just fillers. I think birthdays are coded the same way to help obscure anything he was trying to hide. On top of that, he also included real phone numbers, so if you were to work your way through them all, some would be answered by a person with the correct initials.'

'And you managed to figure all this out in the last 15 minutes?'

'No, silly. I knew where he hid it. Worked the basics out a couple of years ago. I didn't expect to need it, mind, it was more of a mental challenge. The major flaw that I can see is that anyone in the book can reverse engineer the code from their own data.'

'Just as well you did,' said Mads as they reached the corner and turned right. They carried on until they arrived at a sign that read 2120-2140 with an arrow pointing right. They found 2136 and Lyndsey turned the wheels on the padlock. It snapped open with a satisfying click. She pocketed the lock and raised the shutter.

'Gloves on,' she whispered to Mads once they had walked in and lowered the shutter halfway so they wouldn't be seen rooting through everything by a casual passerby.

She switched on the light and they both perused the storage space. Boxes were stacked against each wall.

'This could take ages.'

'Believe it or not, things aren't as bad as they appear. At the back are tees and sweats. He takes a few out at a time and one of his mates screen prints them for him. Beneath those, are his precious magazines. On the left are records. He doesn't take vinyl to the market unless some-one orders something specific from his list. To the right, are the CDs he didn't take with him Saturday. In front of those are various shipping cartons, leaving us with those scruffy looking boxes.'

She indicated to the back corner and gave Mads a big grin.

An hour later, neither of them felt like grinning. They had rummaged through ten boxes and found nothing except old invoices and rubbish he'd become too attached to to throw out. Old concert programmes, ticket stubs, school sports trophies, hideous wall ornaments and other general paraphernalia.

'I remember some of this stuff from when I moved in.

You wouldn't believe the fuss he made when I demanded he threw it out to make room for some of my things. Shall we treat ourselves to something to eat before we meet John in The Pye?'

'That sounds like a good idea. I need to drink something as well, to clear the dust and dirt from my throat after sorting through all that rubbish.'

They left the lockup and Lyndsey wiped the padlock and the pull bar on the shutter with her gloves to remove any fingerprints before putting the lock into place and clicking it shut. She spun the dials a few times to randomise the numbers and they headed for the exit.

They walked into The Pye at 6.45 and after tasting three ales they didn't know, decided what they wanted and ordered a pint each. Three men stood at the bar in conversation while in one of the pub corners as they turned round was a man typing away on a laptop. They headed for the other corner, by the window. If not for the sounds of Black Sabbath in the background the place would have been funereal.

'Quiet night,' said Mads.

'Monday's a bit slow, I think. They don't show live football here either, so anyone wanting to watch that will go elsewhere.'

'Yes, maybe things will liven up later.'

At 7.15 John walked through the door, looked around and came over to their table.

'Hi, sorry I'm late. I got held up.'

'No problem,' said Mads. 'Do you want a drink?'

'No thanks, I imagine there will be alcohol at the game so I don't want to start now.'

'OK, here's the money,' she said sliding an envelope across the table towards him.

'I'll try not to lose it all.'

'Don't worry too much if you do. Better you win, of course, but it wouldn't be the end of the world. We think Barry was a regular on Thursdays, so if you're going to namedrop he was with you when Tibor met you all.'

'Fair enough. I'll do my best. Are you both fit? They said 7.30 to 8.00 so we might as well go now if you're fit.'

Black Sabbath had finished and the barman replaced the CD with another. The opening strains of Hotel California wafted across the pub.

'If I wasn't ready before, I am now,' she said, draining her glass with one fluid movement.

'Not a fan?' asked John.

'Don't set her off,' said Mads. 'She uses The Eagles as a filtration process.'

'A what?'

'When guys start chatting you up, they will tell you anything they think you want to hear. Lyndsey always puts on her sweet little "butter wouldn't melt in my mouth" voice and asks if they like The Eagles. The moment they say yes, they're dead in the water.'

'Based on that?'

'It's sound scientific principle,' said Lyndsey. 'If they're telling the truth they have appalling taste. If they're lying, why do I want to waste my time on them in the first place?'

'That's a little harsh. How about you, Mads? Where do you stand on The Eagles?'

'I've not had much of an opportunity to listen to them. An ex-boyfriend gave me a copy of the Hotel California album once, but I made the mistake of playing it in the car with Lyndsey. It took maybe twenty seconds or so for her to find the eject button and refashion the CD as a frisbee.'

'And not once have you thanked me,' said Lyndsey with a wry smile on her face.

Mads finished her drink and they made their way outside.

'Where is the game?' she asked.

'Along the Brent. Tibor said we'll know it when we see it.'

They walked to Brentford Bridge and made their way down the stairs to the towpath. It was poorly lit and they let John take the lead. Houseboats lined the riverside, but the three of them kept their distance from the edge, not wanting to risk slipping on the damp ground. The path narrowed as they reached a corner, forcing them into single file.

'I wish the towpath was lit better,' said Lyndsey.

'If you walk along the Thames to Richmond, the part between Twickenham and Richmond Bridges is beautifully illuminated, but from Twickenham Bridge all the way back to Kew, not at all,' said John.

'Lighting for the rich, screw the likes of us, eh?'

'I'm not sure that's how the councils word it, but I prefer your version.'

They rounded another corner past a gangplank with a bicycle secured to one of the metal handrails.

'It must be lovely to live on a boat,' said Mads. 'The feeling of freedom, though if I did I'm sure I'd find myself shackled to one place so I'd be no freer.'

'Yes, great idea for a holiday but I don't fancy it as a lifestyle,' said Lyndsey over her shoulder.

They rounded another corner and Lyndsey almost tripped on a wooden jetty that jutted out across the pathway.

'Careful,' said Mads. 'We don't want to fish you out of the water in this weather.'

'It's only about four feet deep so aside from getting cold and wet you should survive,' said John.

'Are you sure?' asked Lyndsey, peering into the black water.

'So I was told when I took one of those guided walks. He was talking about the Grand Union Canal the other side of the bridge, though. Where this is both the canal and the river Brent, things might be different here. I wouldn't suggest jumping in to check.'

'Don't worry, nothing was further from my mind.'

The path widened again and Mads caught up with Lyndsey so they could walk together.

'Some of these boats are pretty, aren't they? Look at this one. I love the white paint and plants growing on the roof.'

She pointed at the California fuchsias hanging down the side, arranged so they didn't block any light coming through the portholes. They reached another bend in the river where a red and yellow barge was moored.

'Oh what a beauty. Just like a floating Swiss chalet.'

'You can ooh and ah all you like. I don't imagine for a moment you'll be giving up your gorgeous house to live on a boat, however charming it may look.'

'Spoilsport, let a girl dream, why don't you.'

They reached some stairs and a sign that read, 'Pedestrians This Way'. Five metres past the steps sat the most utilitarian craft they had ever seen. Made of slate grey metal and shaped like a box on a floating base, it was every bit what one might expect of a boat designed by the team behind the Trabant. A pair of eyes were painted on its flat bow and two muscular men stood by the gangplank.

'I think this might be the one,' said John as they approached the men.

'Is this where we find Tibor?' he asked.

The man closest to him indicated towards the boat with his head but made no effort to move out of the way.

'So can we go in?'

'A luvnyák kint maradnak.'

John smiled at him. 'They're my lucky mascots.'

The man remained impassive with his arms folded across his chest.

'What if they want to play?'

The man turned to his colleague and muttered some-thing. They both burst into laughter. He turned back to face John, his jocular expression disappearing. He nodded towards the women.

'A luvnyák maradnak.'

John turned to them.

'They won't let you on board. What do you want to do?'

'We'll go back to the pub,' said Mads. 'Any idea when you'll be finished?'

'The alarm on my phone is set for eleven, so not long after that. Where will you be, The Pye again?'

'No,' said Lyndsey. 'We'll go to The Droop. At least that might be an Eagles free environment.'

'Fair enough, Expect me about 11.30. Wish me luck.'

They both did and walked back to the metal steps.

'Back the way we came or up and round the pretty way?' asked Mads.

'Let's take the stairs.'

The steps led to a path two metres above the towpath. Looking over the metre high concrete wall separating them from the drop, Lyndsey saw John disappearing into the grey box. They walked alongside a hedge with varying shades of yellow and green leaves through an S shaped bend where they crossed a wooden bridge with handrails. More steps took them to a building that appeared to be a warehouse or workshop judging by the shuttered door. They turned off the river before a road bridge then right underneath it before walking around the edge of the market and past the new social housing estate that had been built five years earlier. As they rounded a long corner in the road, the pub sign came into view and they climbed the small flight of stairs to the Brewer's Droop.

The barman appeared startled to see them when they opened the door. The only customers, a man and woman in conversation and a man perched on a stool doing a crossword didn't even acknowledge their entrance. After a few seconds of peering at them like an inquisitive meer-kat, he greeted them and asked what they wanted. They bought a pint of Buttcombe each and walked through to the other bar where a pool table took up much of the available space. Another door in the corner led outside, a relic from the days when pubs were split into saloon and public bars.

'Fancy a game?' asked Mads.

'Sure, it must be my turn to win one.'

Three games later, Lyndsey figured things didn't work like that and sat down while Mads bought more beer. She brought them back and slumped next to her on the bench seat behind the table. A man approached the table.

'Are you two ladies here for the quiz?'

Lyndsey looked at Mads and screwed up her nose.

'Not tonight, thanks.'

'OK, if you're sure.'

He walked back through to the other bar.

'You didn't want to, did you?' asked Lyndsey.

'No, maybe another time. We can earwig on the questions, gauge our likely chances for another night. I wonder how my money's getting on.'

'I'm sure it's doing fine. John didn't seem nervous.'

'Yes, not sure if that should worry me or not. I wish I could play poker.'

'We wouldn't get past the doormen. What language was he speaking, do you think?'

'No idea, ask John when he gets here. He understood the gist, at least.'

'It didn't sound too complimentary, whatever it was. I'm sure I could take a stab at what he said to his mate.'

'Haha, yes I think we could both guess that comment.'

The pub door opened and a man and woman entered. They walked past the pool table towards the bar but stopped at their table.

'Mads? Is that you? Wow, how long has it been?'

She stared for a few moments.

'Pete, what are you doing here? How are you keeping?'

'I'm fine. Let me order a couple of drinks and we can catch up, if you're not busy, of course?'

'No, not at all. This is Lyndsey, I'm not sure if you ever met. Lyndsey, this is Pete. He was in my art class at uni.'

'Hi , this is Jen, my partner. Grab a chair, I'll get us a drink.'

Jen sat down and smiled.

'How do you know Pete?' asked Mads.

'We both rent studios on Johnson's Island. With only a walkway between us, one thing led to another and here we are.'

'So you're an artist too? What style do you work in?'

'A mixture of experimental paintings and clay or papier mâché sculptures. Dragons are my favourites. They sell quite well at markets and fairs, though most of my income is derived from commissions to model people's departed pets.'

'I love dragons. I must make a point of coming to the next open day. Have you ever been to one, Lynds?'

'Yes, I reported on last November's. There is such an interesting diversity of styles amongst all the artists.'

Pete sat down at the table and passed Jen her drink.

'So Mads, what are you up to? Still painting, I hope?'

Mads looked shamefaced for a moment.

'Not for ages. Lyndsey was trying to talk me into taking it up again.'

'You should, you've got real talent. It's such a waste.'

'I'll think about it. What are you working on now? Still one for the expansive landscapes and unicorns?'

'Over the last year I've got into sci-fi style planets-capes and underwater seascapes. I have an exhibition coming up in Hoxton in a few weeks if you want to come.'

He searched in his pockets and handed her a flyer.

'If I'm not busy I'll be there. Jen tells us you both rent studios on the island.'

'Yes, if you're not busy tomorrow morning we could show you our spaces. We get here about ten so we can meet you outside here. If you're not doing anything, of course. It's not a very sociable time if you have day jobs.'

'What do you reckon, Lynds? We don't have any plans for the morning do we?'

'None I can think of. It might make for a pleasant distraction from everything.'

'It's a date,' said Pete. 'We'll see you both outside the pub at ten.'

The four of them chatted for a couple of hours until Pete and Jen went home. At 10.45 Lyndsey's phone rang. She glanced at it and took the call.

'Hi Grandad.'

'Hello, love. Inspector Savage was round asking for you. He said to go and see him at the police station tomorrow morning about ten.'

'Oh, did he say what it was about?'

'No, he was vague. He's still sitting in his car outside though, so you might want to stay at Mads' house tonight in case he decides to catch you off your guard.'

'Yes, I will. Thanks for calling.'

'No problem. Ring me if you need anything.'

'Will do, goodnight.'

'You too, love. See you tomorrow.'

She put the phone back in her pocket.

'Damn, Savage wants me at the police station tomorrow at ten. Can I stay round yours, please? Grandad says he's still hanging around outside.'

'Of course you can. Did he say what he wanted?'

'No, but I bet he found my watch. Still, nothing I can do now.'

'Oh, Lynds. Maybe you should have gone back for it.'

'I doubt it would matter. He'd have only pulled me in earlier.'

'I'll tell you what. Call me when you get out. If I don't hear from you by eleven, I'll phone our solicitor and ask if she can come down and spring you.'

Lyndsey laughed. 'Spring me? You make me sound like a career criminal.'

'Learn the lingo, girl. You'll need it in pokey.'

They both laughed and chatted about nothing in particular until 11.20 when John walked through the door and strolled across to the table.

'Hi,' he said as he sat down. 'Here you go, Mads.'

He passed her an envelope.

'Did I get my money back?'

'Better, I think it came to about £850.'

'Wow! I'm guessing you're good.'

He laughed. 'Good enough to recognise when I'm being hustled. Let me win a little tonight and next week, then my luck will turn. For what it's worth, I don't think they killed Barry, when I asked about him they said he plays on Thursdays. From their expressions I think he's too much of a cash cow for them to kill him.'

'That's a shame. What language were they speaking?'

'Hungarian. My wife comes from Budapest so I've picked up a few phrases.'

'I got the impression they were saying things she isn't likely to.'

'Well, yes, but whatever the Daily Mail might try to tell you, it isn't only Poles we get at the builders' merchants. And I'm scheduled to open up in the morning so I'll head off. If you need anything else, give me a call.'

'Don't you want some of the winnings?'

'No, you keep it. I'll go back next week and let them think they've hooked a sucker. See you around.'

Mads put the envelope into her bag and turned to Lyndsey. 'I'll best get you home so you're refreshed and awake for the inspector in the morning. Wait here, I'll ask the barman to call us a cab.'

Mads climbed out of bed at five o'clock next morning and crept downstairs. After making a pot of coffee, she sat at the computer and inserted Lyndsey's USB stick. She copied the zzzz.zip file to her desktop, then right-clicked and selected Extract all. A password window popped up. She picked up Barry's book and flicked straight to the Zs, finding it empty.

OK, Barry. Attrition it is.

She turned to the start and began the painstaking process of trying each number sequence in order. Three mugs of coffee and almost two hours later, she stumbled on the correct entry, "Sid 7Ø81624/8299467/777856Ø730★".

Once the zip file had finished unpacking, she found a directory on her desktop containing a few files and multiple other directories. Her eyes locked on the one titled LyndseyM.

Inside, Mads found a wealth of information. Pictures, log-ins, copies of emails and monthly reports dating back the three years since he had known Lyndsey. The reports all focussed on her parents, and any mentions she had made of them, both to him and those he'd overheard during conversations with Bert.

She started wondering if he was an undercover policeman. There had been a huge outcry a couple of years earlier when covert officers had been outed from deep cover when they had set up home with animal rights activists. Some had even had families with those who they had been investigating. That didn't ring true, though. If he had been an undercover cop, Brentford would be swarming with detectives and investigators. The death of any cop would warrant a far more high profile investigation than Inspector Savage.

She came out of Lyndsey's directory and scanned the names of the others. She recognised a couple such as Bert and Bob and opened their directories, just to check it was them. Although the personal information he had on them was limited, he had been collecting it longer. The dates on the reports preceded the opening of Brentford market by a few years.

She wondered how old Barry was. She had assumed he was about the same age as Lyndsey, but this made her wonder if he had been a little older. Not too much, but thirty-five, perhaps?

He had been technically adept, somehow managing to compile lists of phone calls and emails. She checked the directory names and found he also had one on Jools, under her real name of Julie containing similar. The monthly reports, however, weren't interested in them at all, just in any contact with those involved in animal rights and mentions of Lyndsey's parents. There was no indication of where he had sent them. As someone with the technical know-how to gather this much information, Barry ensured he allowed no one else the same opportunity.

She opened a directory of someone she didn't recognise the name of at random. He had nothing to do with animal rights, and judging by his photograph, Mads wondered if this was one of Barry's "friends" Ranjit had spoken about. He was an unsavoury type of character judging by his reports.

In other directories were incriminating photos of people having affairs and a couple of politicians taking bribes. It was interesting that those directories contained no reports at all. Just a few notes to place the pictures into context.

What if Barry was a private investigator and a blackmailer? It was a possibility from the evidence she was hunting through, but she had no way of checking. Successive Governments had talked about licensing the PI industry for years but, as far as she knew, had never got around to finalising the legislation and making it law. On top of that, even if there was an Association of British Blackmailers, it was unlikely their records were public.

She shut down the computer. It was almost eight o'clock, and she needed to wake Lyndsey and cook some breakfast for them both if she was going to meet Savage at ten. She pondered over whether she should tell the police about her findings. If Barry had been a blackmailer, the potential suspects for his murder had expanded, and there was little she could do to investigate any of them. But how would she explain how she came across the information without incriminating them both in compromising a crime scene? Not to mention, deleting the file from Barry's computer.

She decided to leave it for now, and there was no way she was ready to tell Lyndsey about the seeming interest in her parents, or their remarkable regeneration.

Something was afoot, and she needed more information before she could make a decision.

37

Having seen Lyndsey off on the 237 bus, Mads strolled along the river towards Brentford. The brisk wind buffeting her face was refreshing and with her blonde hair streaming behind her as she walked, she visualised herself as a rock star filming a video. The diverse array of water craft moored next to the park would have provided an interesting backdrop. She wondered what this stretch would be like in a couple of years when the leisure centre would be replaced with overpriced riverside flats and the boats evicted by the council to make way for a marina. Brentford was changing fast, and she wasn't sure it was for the best.

Only after a concerted local campaign had the market and social housing been approved six years ago, else that land would have also been transformed into expensive flats and offices, detracting further from the community feel that had always engendered the residents to the town.

She thought about the case. For all their investigating, they didn't seem to be getting anywhere. Was it likely Bill and Rhonda killed Barry? They had a clear motive through Sharon and she was sure they could have slipped across and taken the knife without being noticed, but still. They didn't come across as killers. Not that she had any real life experience of meeting murderers, but there would be something. Nerves or uncertainty perhaps. And Lyndsey had been certain they had no blood on them. She took out her phone and found Sharon's number in the history.

'Hello?'

'It's Mads. The reporter from yesterday.'

'Hi.'

'Did your parents know about your pregnancy?'

Sharon gasped.

'No, please don't tell them anything or put it in the paper. They'll kill me if they find out.'

'Don't worry, I wasn't going to. I just needed to check.'

'You promise you won't tell anyone?'

'Your secret's safe with me. I didn't mean to panic you.'

'Thank you. Any news on who killed him yet?'

'No, but we're making progress.'

'Good luck, is there anything else?'

'No, that's all. Sorry to trouble you again.'

If she was right about them not knowing, that took away Bill and Rhonda's motive. And it also meant she was no further forward in finding out who killed him.

She walked up the gentle slope to the High Street at the end of the park and carried on along the pavement for a few hundred metres until she turned left into a cobbled brick road opposite the supermarket. She stopped to watch the water gushing across the weir, allowing the sound to relax her. She had photographed this for a project at uni and with a little judicious editing in Photoshop had managed to crop the image to make it look like an ideal spot for high speed canoeing. After titling the photo Brentford Rapids, she had found it funny when a small group in her class spent an entire weekend looking for the location. To this day, Mads and Lyndsey were the only ones who knew the truth.

No, she was wrong in thinking they were no further forward. Being able to eliminate Bill and Rhonda was reductive progress as it took away a possible line of enquiry. The same could be said for the Hungarian card sharps and those he had owed money to. The problem was, with the exception of any blackmail victims, no one had compelling reason to kill him. She was certain someone wasn't telling them something.

She walked on towards a housing estate, turning off just before it to cross a bridge across a lock, then on to another that crossed the 'rapids'. This led to a small alleyway that passed the gate to Johnson's Island and another small bridge which took her to the Droop. Pete and Jen were outside the pub waiting.

'Sorry, am I late?'

Pete smiled. 'No, we're early. We only just got here so don't worry. Where's Lyndsey? Isn't she coming?'

'She had something come up, but she promised to come to the next open day.'

Mads followed them back over the small bridge and through the slatted gate which led to a small yard. As they passed a tree, she could see the doors to a couple of small studios on her right and another to her left, next to the main building they were heading for. Just inside the front door, she saw an artist in a small studio to the left working on a painting with her back to them. They followed a small corridor and climbed some stairs. At the top, they walked through a doorway and Pete turned to face Mads.

'These are our studios. If you imagine a walkway through the middle of the room, then Jen works on the left and I'm on the right.'

'Shame you don't have any windows, the view must be lovely in the summer.'

'Some of the others do, but they're smaller. I think on balance I prefer the extra space and no distractions.'

Mads admired their work and chatted until her phone alarm beeped.

'Eleven o'clock. I must make a call, OK if I go out to the yard for a couple of minutes?'

'Yes, of course. I'll make some coffee while you're gone, would you like one?'

'Please,' she said. 'Black, no sugar. Back in a mo.'

Mads made her way down and out the door. She marvelled at how peaceful it was. The sound of the weir obscured the noise of traffic from the nearby High Street, and it was easy to believe she was in a small village miles from London. Standing beneath the tree she called her solicitor and filled her in on Lyndsey's plight. She promised to go to Hounslow police station at once to see what she could do.

Mads removed the phone from her ear and took a refreshing breath of air. Hearing a movement behind her she made to turn round.

Then her world went black.

38

Lyndsey arrived in Hounslow at 9.50 and went straight to the police station. After a five minute wait, Savage appeared with a folder in his hand and led her through to an interview room.

'Take a seat, Lyndsey,' he said indicating a chair.

He walked around the table, sat down and stared at her for a few moments before pressing a switch.

'For the record my name is Inspector Samuel Savage. I am interviewing Miss Lyndsey Marshall regarding the murder of Barry Williams at Brentford Market on Saturday, 10th October. The time is ...' he checked his watch, '... 9.57 on Tuesday, 13th October. Ms Marshall, you are not being formally charged with anything at this stage, but should you be charged at a later time or date it may harm your defence if you do not mention, when questioned, something you later rely on in court. Anything you do say may be given in evidence. Do you understand?'

She took a deep breath and tried to appear as relaxed as possible.

'Yes, but I've done nothing wrong.'

'Could you confirm for me, Ms Marshall, that you are here of your own free will for the purposes of this interview?'

'Did I have a choice?'

Savage looked at her across the table. 'I could arrest you if that makes it easier for you, Lyndsey. Would you rather I did that?'

She stared down at the table for a few moments. 'No, let's get this over with.'

'Could you answer the question, please?'

'I confirm I am here of my own free will.'

'Thank you.'

He took a picture from the folder and slid it across the table towards her.

'Do you recognise that room?'

She studied the photo.

'It's the bedroom in my old flat.'

'Do you notice anything about it?'

'Nothing unusual. What am I looking for?'

'You see the time and date at the bottom?'

'Yes, 15.23, Saturday. What about it?'

He produced another and laid it next to the first.

'Do you recognise that room?'

'It's the same bedroom, from a different angle.'

'And what do you notice about this one?'

'It was taken yesterday at 17.13?'

'Anything else?'

She shrugged.

'It looks the same to me.'

He stared at her in silence for a few moments.

'You don't see that?' he said pointing to the floor next to the bedside table.

'Oh yes, what is it?' she asked, knowing the answer full well.

Savage produced a plastic evidence bag from the folder and slid it across the table.

'Have you seen this watch before?'

Lyndsey picked the bag up and inspected it carefully.

'It's mine. I wondered where that was. Where did you find it?'

He pointed back to the second picture.

'Would you care to explain to me how your watch appeared in your old flat between Saturday afternoon and Monday evening despite the door being secured with police tape?'

Lyndsey opened her eyes wide in what she hoped was

an innocent pose.

'How would I know? I must have left it behind when I moved out.'

Savage sighed. 'Yet it was nowhere to be seen on Saturday.'

'I don't know what to tell you.'

'Do you have a set of keys on you?'

'Yes, of course.' Lyndsey took a keyring from her pocket and passed it across the table, thanking her lucky stars she'd remembered to remove Barry's that morning.'

He compared the keys with some from the folder before handing them back.

'I don't believe you.'

She shrugged. 'How would I get in? I handed the keys back to him when I left.'

'Yet there were only a single set on his person and no others in the flat. How do you explain that?'

'Maybe he gave them to another one of his girl-friends? Maybe you didn't search hard enough? Maybe you found the watch somewhere else and planted it your-self to give you an excuse to question me? I thought it was your job to solve puzzles like this, not mine.'

He shook his head.

'Miss Marshall. I'm going to have a word with my custody sergeant and ask him to find you a nice, comfortable cell to sit in while you reconsider your answers. I warn you, I'm tempted to charge you with compromising a crime scene. That is a serious crime which could have huge repercussions for you in the future. I suggest you use the time to think very hard about how you want to play this.'

He put everything back into the folder and stood.

'Do you have anything you want to tell me?'

Lyndsey shook her head.

'Interview terminated at 10.06,' he said before pressing the switch again and leaving the room. After a few minutes, a policewoman entered the room with a plastic bag.

'Could you stand and empty your pockets on the table, please?' she said.

Lyndsey did as she was asked then allowed the woman to pat her down. The policewoman placed each item into the bag, stating out loud what everything was as she wrote the items down. When she had finished, she gave Lyndsey the sheet of paper to sign and placed it in the property bag before sealing it. She led her to a stark cell and slammed the door shut.

She lay on the bench seat in the cell and stared up at the ceiling. Knowing this was a psychological ploy made it no less unsettling. The lack of visual stimuli in the small, grey room was making her mind race and she fought against the feelings of panic that were threatening to take hold. She closed her eyes and took a deep breath.

Don't worry, Mads will call the solicitor and she'll get you out of this. Relax and stay calm until she gets here.

She started to sort through the events of the past few days. So much had happened and they seemed no closer to finding out who had killed Barry. She found it difficult to believe that Bill and Rhonda could do such a thing. She didn't know them as well as she knew Bob and Jools, but they didn't fit her preconceptions of a murderer. Then again, what was the type? Murderers didn't have KILLER tattooed on their foreheads. The problem was that every other path they had followed had led to a dead end. They had to be missing something obvious, but what?

She was no closer to solving the conundrum when a key was pushed into the door. She sat up as the door swung open and a woman in a grey business suit thanked the officer and walked into the cell. The door slammed shut behind her.

'Hello, I'm guessing you must be Lyndsey. My name's Margaret. Mads asked me to come and help you. The desk sergeant filled me in with the basics but I need your side of the story. Why are you sitting here?'

'The inspector thinks I broke into my ex-boyfriend's flat and compromised a crime scene.'

'I assume you denied the accusation.'

'Yes.'

'Good, so what is he basing this on? Does he have any evidence?'

'He says he found my watch in the bedroom yesterday and it wasn't there on Saturday.'

'How do you account for it being there?'

'When I moved out I must have left it behind.'

'OK, and it is your watch?'

'Yes, my name's engraved on the back.'

'Do you have keys to the property?'

'No, he checked my keys and they didn't match.'

'So how does he think you got in?'

Lyndsey shrugged. 'He didn't say.'

'Why did you break up with, Barry is it?'

'I caught him with another girl. It turns out she wasn't the only one either.'

'So fidelity isn't his strong suit.'

'No, and I feel like an idiot for not noticing anything.'

'Don't blame yourself, Lyndsey, you're not at fault.'

She smiled. 'Thanks, but that's how it seems to me.'

'I think I have enough here. Are you ready to go out and talk to the inspector again? He'll be wanting to ask the same questions as he did earlier, hoping you slip up. Stay calm and answer them. If he asks anything that seems out of order, I'll step in. If I take the lead, sit quiet and roll with it. Any questions?'

Lyndsey shook her head. 'Sounds fine to me.'

Margaret walked over to the door and rang the bell. After a minute or two they heard the key in the lock once more.

'We're ready for Inspector Savage now,' she said to the officer.

He led the way to the same interview room Lyndsey had been in before but an extra chair had appeared for Margaret. After another couple of minutes, Inspector Savage entered the room and nodded to the officer who closed the door on his way out. Savage sat down and placed the file on the desk. He pressed the switch and once again announced the date, time and the names of those present for the benefit of the tape.

'So, Lyndsey, have you had enough time to reconsider your answers?'

Margaret held a hand up. 'For the sake of making sure we're all on the same page, Inspector, would it be possible to start from scratch?'

He sighed, then opened the file.

'This is a picture of Barry Williams' bedroom taken Saturday afternoon. This is another picture of the same room from Monday afternoon.'

He pushed the photos across the desk.

'They are almost identical aside from one small detail.' He removed the watch from the file with a flourish. 'This watch has appeared in the room despite the flat being marked as a crime scene with police tape. The back of the watch is engraved with the name Lyndsey and Miss Marshall confirms it belongs to her. I am trying to ascertain how it got there.'

'I see, and you have a witness to confirm that my client entered the premises at some point between Saturday and Monday?'

'No, but ...'

'I believe my client also told you she has not seen the watch since she moved out and that she assumes she left it in the flat when leaving?'

'That is her story, yes.'

'I also believe you checked her keyring and can therefore confirm she is not carrying keys to the property.'

'Not now she isn't, but she could have hidden them somewhere.'

'Is anything missing from the property, or been disturbed during the period in question?'

'Not that I noticed, no.'

'Inspector, you appear to be on a fishing expedition. May I present to you two scenarios, then you tell me which is the most likely?'

'If you must.'

'Lyndsey here, transports herself through a locked door with no one seeing her, then, without disturbing anything, places a watch—a watch with her name on no less—where she knows it will be seen. She then disappears, again with not one witness.

'Or let's investigate another possibility. As she claims, Lyndsey forgot to take the watch with her when she moved out, leaving her keys with Barry. From what I understand, Mr Williams was something of a lady's man, so it's not too much of a leap to imagine he handed the keys to another of his girlfriends. Now, just supposing, she came across Lyndsey's watch and assumed that Lyndsey was another woman muscling in on her territory. When Barry is found dead, she senses an opportunity to get revenge for Lyndsey cheating with her man, and slips back into the flat to put the watch somewhere she knows you will find it. Which of those two do you imagine a court would believe, Inspector?'

'You're twisting the evidence.'

'Evidence? I see no evidence of my client's involvement at all, Inspector. May I remind you that under English law, your suspicions do not constitute evidence, however inventive and entertaining they might be. Lyndsey told you she lost the watch and is grateful you have found it. I don't believe you have any other grounds to speak to her at this point.'

He sighed. 'Just for the record, Ms Marshall, when was the last time you saw this watch before today?'

'Before I moved out of Barry's flat.'

'And you left your set of keys with Barry when you moved?'

'Yes, I did.'

'And you still maintain you have not returned to the flat since that day.'

'I do.'

'Then I have no need to detain you any longer, Miss Marshall. I will hold on to the watch for DNA testing in case there is any trace of this 'other woman' on it and I will also be asking neighbours if they saw anyone in the vicinity those two days. If, as I still believe, it was you who entered the flat, you had best hope the neighbours are either unobservant or very forgetful.'

He terminated the recording and gathered everything together before walking to the door and holding it open.

'After you, ladies. If you make your way along the corridor the desk sergeant will show you out. Have a good day.'

Lyndsey collected her belongings and walked outside with Margaret.

'Thank you, I could have been locked up for hours.'

'You're welcome. Hopefully, you won't need me again, but if you do here's my card. Mads told me to tell you that she will take care of any billing.'

'Oh, she shouldn't. I'll sort that out with her.'

'It's been a pleasure to meet you Lyndsey and I hope your life starts to look up.'

They shook hands and Margaret walked away. Lyndsey headed for the bus stop, phoning Mads on the way. The call went to voicemail.

'Hey Mads. Thanks for Margaret. She sprung me, as

you put it. Making my way back now. Let me know where to find you.'

She dropped the phone into her pocket and seeing the 237 coming along the road, broke into a run for the bus stop.

Lyndsey got off the bus at Brentford High Street and rang
Mads again, again getting voicemail. She decided to make
her way to Johnson's Island to see if Pete and Jen had any
idea where she had got to.

The gate was locked and the Island appeared unin-
habited judging by what she could see through the slats,
so she hung around outside browsing her phone until a
man with a shaved head and wearing a Hawaiian shirt
approached.

'Excuse me,' she said. 'I was meant to be meeting with
Pete and Jen but I've mislaid their number. I don't suppose
you could let me in?'

He looked her up and down.

'I know them. Follow me.'

He opened the gate and Lyndsey followed him
through the courtyard.

'Wait here,' he said when they were inside the building. 'I'll go and check they're in.'

She looked around. To her left and right were closed doors. One looked like a storage cupboard, but she assumed the other was a studio. After a few moments, Hawaiian shirt man reappeared.

'Come through, they're upstairs.'

She followed him round the tiny corridor and climbed the stairs he indicated. Pete was standing at the top.

'Hi, Lyndsey. We thought you were going to be Mads.'

'Oh, is she not here?'

'She was, but she went outside to phone somebody. She was planning to come back because I made her a coffee, but she never did so we assumed that something had happened that caused her to rush off.'

Lyndsey took a deep breath. Something was wrong, the call must have been to Margaret and there would have been no reason for Mads to disappear, so where was she?

'Are you OK? Come through and sit down, I'll make you a coffee.'

She followed and said 'hello' to Jen before sitting in a chair Pete found her.

'How do you take it?'

'Black, no sugar, please.'

He went to make the drinks and Jen walked across.

'Where did Mads run off to? Do you have any idea?'

Lyndsey shook her head. 'No, and she's not answering her phone. I was hoping to find her here.'

'How strange. She went to make a call and never came back.'

'So Pete said. I hope she's OK.'

'Oh, I'm sure she is. I bet she got called away and the door locked behind her so she couldn't tell us. Reception in here can be sketchy with the trees.'

'Yes, I'm sure that's what happened,' said Lyndsey, not believing a word.

Pete came back with the coffee which she drank whilst looking at their creations. She made appreciative noises, but was too distracted to concentrate. After half an hour, she made her excuses and headed back down the stairs and out the door.

Lyndsey rang Mads again once she was outside. From somewhere close a ringtone sounded. The call went to voicemail, so she hung up and called again. The sound was coming from a pile of leaves that had collected next to some old wooden planks leant against a tree branch. She hunted through and found Mads' phone.

No wonder there had been no answer. Now, where is she?

41

Mads came to with a splitting headache, feeling groggy and nauseated. Her eyes shot open as she struggled to draw breath. She closed her eyes again while she took a couple of deep breaths through her nose to try to calm herself down a little.

She couldn't feel her right arm at all, so tried to shift her body weight off it. As she did, the painful stab of pins and needles made her want to cry out, but the tape across her mouth prevented her from doing so. Her hands were taped behind her back and her legs were also bound together. All she could smell was paint fumes and old carpet, which was what she guessed was rolled around her blocking most of the light. Mads heard muffled movement from the room and decided to lie still in case whoever it was realised she was conscious.

She blinked her eyes in an attempt to stop shapes

dancing in front of them. It didn't work. She moved her head back and pain shot through her body as the back of her head touched the carpet.

Wow, someone must have hit me from behind. I bet my hair's in a right mess. I should get to a hospital. Or a hairdressers. Better still, a hospital with a hairdressers.

She tried thinking back to the last thing she remembered. She had walked outside to phone Margaret, then nothing. She heard a ringtone and a muffled voice. It was a woman but she didn't recognise the voice through the carpet.

'Hang on, I'll come and let you in.'

She heard the door open and slam shut. Mads tried to manoeuvre herself into a more comfortable position. Five minutes later, whoever it was returned and she lay still once more.

'You're joking, right? In that old rug?'

'I saw her enter in the mirror and panicked, OK?'

'But she's a reporter. She could be here for anything.'

'No she isn't. I phoned the local papers. None of them have heard of her.'

'So, is she ...?'

'Yes ... no ... I don't know. I'm not unwrapping her to find out. She needs to be moved from here regardless.'

There was a pause.

'Well, Brentford are at home tonight, so we can't do anything before eight. There will be too many people about.'

'Thanks, I'll make it up to you.'

The door opened and closed again and after listening for a couple of minutes She figured she was alone and started to try to free herself.

After a good hour of squirming and pushing, Mads had stretched the bindings on the rug enough to move her knees up to her chest. She was now confined so tightly that it hampered her breathing, but kept trying until she managed to loop her hands over her feet. She stopped to take some deep breaths before managing to straighten her legs out again, leaving her hands in front of her.

Sliding her bound wrists up her body was easier said than done. After what seemed like an eternity, she had raised them high enough to pick at the tape covering her mouth. It was wrapped around her head two or three times so it wasn't a case of just peeling it off. She managed to unstick the bottom edge from her chin and rolled it up, sticking it on itself so it didn't slip down again.

That bitch is going to pay for this. I'll never get this crap out of my hair.

Mads screamed long and loud.

Nothing.

She screamed again.

More nothing.

She tried working her hands higher so she could use her teeth to free her wrists. This was more difficult that it had been moving her legs. Her arms and elbows didn't have the strength of her legs and knees. At least they didn't have to move as far. After another ten minutes she had her hands high enough to start nibbling at the tape.

She was making slow progress but a small rip had appeared at the top. She pressed her fists together to lever the tape apart but it wasn't having any of it. She moved her head back to try to get her wrists higher. In the fading light she saw a carrier bag at the end of the tunnel. Despite the pain, she straightened her arms and managed to loop her fingers through the handle, hoping it contained something sharp she could use to cut herself free. She dragged it into the rug and felt its contents through the bag, but there was nothing hard. It felt like old rags that could be used to wipe paintbrushes. She pulled it a little further down and rested her head on it like a pillow, then started chewing at the lower edge of the tape with her teeth, figuring that her arms would be able to give better leverage.

The light faded until she was in darkness. She was bathed in sweat from the exertion and didn't think she had ever been more uncomfortable when she heard a key in the door. She stopped moving and lay quiet.

Damn! Now what?

42

Lyndsey pocketed Mads' phone and went back home. She made herself a quick sandwich, then as an afterthought made another and put it in a bag for later. She slipped that into her jacket pocket before walking through to the front room.

'OK if I borrow the van, Grandad? I need to find Mads and she isn't answering her phone.'

'Of course. Here you go.' He took out his wallet and gave her £60. 'Fill her up with diesel while you're out.'

'Will do. Anything else you want?'

'No thanks. How did your meeting with the police go?'

'I swear he thinks I killed Barry. I'd still be there if Mads hadn't sent her solicitor down to represent me.'

'She's a smart cookie, that Mads. I'll tell you, if I were forty or fifty years younger.'

'Eww, stop it. I don't need that mental image.'

He laughed. 'I wasn't always this old, you know.'

'But you are to me, I'll see you later.'

She went back to the kitchen and made herself a flask of coffee while she ate her sandwich. There were a limited number of places Mads was likely to be and she didn't expect her to be at any of them, so she would need something to drink.

The first place she tried was Mads' house, then popped into her local gym, but the bored looking stick insect behind the desk said she'd not seen her for a couple of weeks. She then drove to Richmond in case she had gone to see Bill and Rhonda again, but drew a blank there too, leaving Lyndsey at a loss for ideas.

She found herself wondering if Mads had burst in and accused the two of them so was now trussed up in the storeroom, but smiled to herself as she discounted the idea. She drove back and parked just past the Droop, then settled low in the driver's seat and got out her e-reader. It was a long shot, but if she was anywhere, Johnson's Island was the most likely place and she was determined to wait until she found her.

A few people came and went over the afternoon but no one out of the ordinary. As the light began to fade around five, Pete and Jen left, then fifteen minutes later the man in the Hawaiian shirt walked past. The pub sounded like it was filling up judging by the sounds of conversations from groups standing outside drinking and smoking. At 7.15, they started trailing off leaving her in peace again. At 7.45 a box van backed down the road, stopping by the pedestrian bridge to Johnson's Island. Lyndsey huddled down further to make sure she was out of sight, though she was sure the reflection of the yellow streetlight on the windscreen would prevent anyone seeing her.

Two people got out of the box van. The driver slid up the shutter at the back and they both walked across the bridge. They were wearing woollen hats pulled down low and their coat collars turned up to obscure their features as much as possible. It might be October but the temperature was mild and she didn't need Mads here to tell her how suspicious that looked. They entered Johnson's Island and shut the gate behind them. Five minutes later, they reappeared carrying a heavy package between them. It looked like a roll of carpet, but she couldn't be sure. They threw it into the back of the box van, closed the shutter and got back in.

Lyndsey sat up and jotted down the registration number. The box van started up again and drew away. After a couple of seconds, she began to follow.

Mads heard the woman's voice again.

'You take that end.'

They both grunted as they lifted the rug.

Gee thanks, I'm not that bloody heavy!

She felt herself being carried outside. It was as much as she could do to not make a noise when she was dropped to the floor by the gates. She soon found herself being lifted again and heard the sound of water as they crossed the bridge. She was in two minds. Should she scream and hope someone was in the Droop who would come to her aid? She thought back to how quiet the pub had been last night before the quiz and decided against it. She also didn't want to make her captors panic with all this water about. She wouldn't take long to drown trussed up as she was. Best bet would be to try to get free once they left her alone and escape from there, wherever it was.

She felt herself thrown into the back of the van and heard the door slide shut. As soon as the cab doors slammed, she set about biting her ties with added fervour. After ten minutes she made a breakthrough and with all her strength tried to prise the tape apart. Nothing gave and she took a couple of deep breaths before trying again. The pressure on her wrists was almost unbearable and she hated to think of the bruises she would be rocking in the morning. Once again, nothing. She closed her eyes and breathed in a few times before putting every gram of energy she had into levering the tape apart. Just as she was going to give up, she felt it give. All at once, with a small ripping sound, her hands were free.

She sighed with relief and started rubbing her hands on her chest as the blood raced into her fingers and the agony of pins and needles made them tender. Once they had stopped hurting, she pushed the carrier bag out of the tube she was in and tried to squeeze herself upwards. It was tied too tightly for her body to fit through the space where her neck had been, so she stretched her right arm to bend her elbow round the top of the rug so she could try to unwind the tape.

After two or three attempts she found the end and unwound it as far as she could. Holding on to it, she tried to roll the rug across the van floor so she could unroll more. It took a concerted effort, but after a few tries, she managed to unstick it enough so the rug unfurled and gave her breathing space. She wriggled out and stood up, rubbing her legs to get the blood flowing.

Now I know what a tube of toothpaste feels like.

Hurtling along the road it was difficult keeping her balance, so she sat down, planning to unwrap the her ankles. As she did she felt the van brake and veer off to the side. Mads edged her way over to the shutter door. She felt around until she found a switch, then waited to come to a stop. They accelerated and the rug and carrier bag slid across the floor towards her. She grabbed the bag and held it between her teeth, thinking that whatever was in there could help identify her captors through DNA tests. If nothing else, it might protect her head if she banged it jumping out.

They were moving slower now, as if in traffic, and she carried on trying to unpick the tape round her ankles. Before she made any more progress, the van eased to a halt. She flicked the door switch, stood to raise the shutter ... and jumped.

Lyndsey drove to the end of the road and followed the box van as it turned right. They both stopped at the red light by The Wasp's Nest, then carried on to the Great West Road where they joined the M4. She let them get a couple of cars in front once they were on the motorway, not wanting to bring attention to herself. They were moving at a steady 50 mph which flew in the face of all the car chases in films, despite not having the hills of San Francisco to contend with. On balance, she figured she preferred this more sedate type chase. It seemed far more English.

They carried on until they reached Junction 6. The box van and the car behind it indicated to leave the motorway and the car in front of Lyndsey moved out to the middle lane to continue. She followed them onto the off ramp. The lights at the bottom were green and they all went through those and the next set. Lyndsey thought she was going to lose them just before the Slough turn off, but put her foot down and hared through the amber light in pursuit just as it changed.

They were lucky with traffic at the next roundabout and continued straight on, but as they reached the next crossroads, the lights turned red and the box van drew to a halt.

All of a sudden the back door was wrenched up and someone with a bag in their mouth leapt onto the bonnet of the car in front of her. The body rolled across the car roof and she glimpsed a flash of blonde hair.

'Mads!' she yelled, and opened her door just as the driver of the car opened his. She jumped out of the van and just managed to catch her as she slithered along the boot.

'Oi, what are you playing at?' shouted the driver. He strutted to the back of his car but after one look at Mads his anger dissipated. 'Are you all right?'

The lights changed and the box van continued on its journey without the driver noticing it had shed its load.

'Are you OK?' asked Lyndsey taking the bag from her mouth and hugging her friend as if she hadn't seen her in years.

Mads nodded. 'Yes, nothing that won't heal. Sorry about your car, I'll give you my number so you can bill me for any damage.'

She fished the notepad and pen from her pocket and scribbled her details down.

'Thanks,' he said. 'Are you sure you're OK? Shall I phone an ambulance?'

'No, I should be fine now, Lyndsey can take care of me. I'd better take your information though, in case the police need a witness.'

He handed over a business card and returned to his car. Lyndsey helped Mads hop to the passenger door and into the van under the gaze of all the motorists who had slowed to a crawl so they could gawk at the action. Lyndsey walked round and climbed back in. Seeing Mads fighting with the tape binding her ankles she opened the glove box.

'Here you go, there are a small pair of scissors in here.' She took them out and handed them across. 'What happened to you?'

'Someone knocked me out cold at Johnson's Island and tied me up in an old rug. Why are you here? Come to that, where are we?'

'We're just outside Slough. When I couldn't contact you, I went to the island thinking you were still with Pete and Jen. I called you again as I left and found your phone in a pile of leaves by the tree.'

'You've got my phone? That's a relief. It must have flown out of my hand when I got hit on the head.'

'I went to get the van and tried everywhere I thought you could be, then sat outside The Droop for hours figuring you must still be on the island. I couldn't think of anything else to do.'

'I'm glad you did. I don't know what I'd have ended up doing. I hadn't planned any further ahead than jumping.'

'Let's find somewhere for you to clean up. What do you think, towards Slough?'

'Anywhere. I'm parched, do you have anything to drink?'

'Coffee?'

'No, I need something cold. If we can stop at a service station and grab something I'll be able to think a little clearer.'

Lyndsey edged the van into the right turn lane, much to the disgruntlement of the drivers behind them. When they reached the next junction she saw a garage and pulled in.

'I have to top up and I'll buy you something cold while I'm in there. Maybe you can use the toilet to clean up?'

Mads glowered at the service station with distaste.

'Most of all, I need to get this sticky tape out of my hair. Why don't we head for Windsor? I know a lovely little hotel nearby.'

'If you say so. What have you got in the bag?'

'Just rags I think. I used it as a pillow then figured it might protect my head if I hit it on something as I jumped out. Plus, whoever it was who kidnapped me might have left some DNA on the material.'

Lyndsey peered into the bag and gasped.

'This isn't old rags and we don't need a DNA test. I know who the killer is.'

As Lyndsey drove to Windsor, Mads made short work of a can of orange and a bottle of water. Refreshed somewhat, she rang Margaret to ask if she would accompany them to see Inspector Savage to hand over the evidence. Margaret suggested it would be a good idea to all have breakfast first, so they could both get the facts straight in their minds before making police statements. They arranged to meet in a small independent café in Runnymede next morning at ten.

Having checked in, Mads spent the best part of two hours in a hot bath soothing her bruises. Having soaked the tape adhesive and resulting sticky mess from her hair, she dried herself off and swaddled herself in a robe before phoning room service and ordering them both a pizza and some wine.

'Are you sure you don't want to go to the hospital?'

asked Lyndsey.

'No, I'm fine. If I get any symptoms I'll tell you, but what I most need is something to eat and a restful night in a comfy bed.'

'As long as you're sure.'

Mads nodded.

'So what's in the bag that's so vital to the case?'

'A Ramones sweatshirt, and judging by what I can see without touching it, it's caked in blood.'

'What's the significance of the Ramones?'

'On Sunday morning Bob and Jools were bickering with each other like they always do. He was adamant that Martin had been wearing a Ramones shirt the day before, while Jools was certain it was the UK Subs. She said she found it funny that he had a C.I.D. shirt on with all the police about. I think they were both right. I bet he wore the Ramones shirt early, then when he got covered in blood, pinched a UK Subs shirt from Barry's stall to wear instead.'

'But why? I don't understand why Martin would do it.'

Lyndsey looked pensive for a moment.

'Nor me, but we had better leave something for the police to do else they'll think we're trying to hog the limelight.'

'Unless ... what if Barry and Mary ...'

Lyndsey sighed. 'Well, at least I'm not going to struggle with hating her, unlike poor Sharon. Carry on.'

'Well, I was thinking. What if he told her his relationship with you was over, assuming she even knew you existed. She watches him come across to your stall to bait you, and figures he probably lied. So they start fighting, Martin ducks across to get the knife—remember Rhonda thought he went for breakfast—comes back and threatens Barry to make him leave Mary alone.'

'So far, so fanciful. Then what?'

'That's it, for the moment. I don't see Martin killing him. He wouldn't have the nerve. And why would Mary help him cover it up? She has no interest in Martin except as a lapdog. Once Barry's dead, if she screams and alerts the entire market, she's got rid of him with none of the blame.'

Lyndsey walked across to the kettle that had just boiled.

'Tea while we wait for the food?'

'Yes, please.'

She made them both a cup while deep in thought.

'Where was Barry stabbed? Which side of his body?'

'Steve said his right side. Why?'

Lyndsey brought the teas over and sat back down on her bed.

'I don't know him, but from what I saw yesterday as they packed up, Martin is right handed.'

'And?'

'Well, where's your drawing of the crime scene?'

Mads took the notepad from her jacket pocket and found the page.

'Now stand between the beds.'

She did as she was told, even though her legs were screaming at her to stay put. Lyndsey stood and took the pad from her.

'So you're Barry and I'm Martin. If I stab you on the right side of your body and stand where the blood gushes all over me—see how I need to twist my arm into an awkward position unless I use my left hand. No one's going to stab someone with their weaker hand are they? But, what if he threatened Barry, Barry laughed at him and dared him to do it. Seeing Martin was about to lose his nerve, Mary grabs the knife and stabs him instead. She might be left handed.'

'I like the way you're thinking. Martin was so close, he gets soaked with blood. They shut Barry in the wardrobe, Mary wipes her hands with his shirt which she hid in a carrier bag and Martin grabbed another one hoping no one would notice. Brilliant!'

'If Bob and Jools hadn't had that silly argument about

his sweatshirt I wouldn't have known it was relevant.'

'And I would never have found it had Mary not panicked when I showed up at Johnson's Island. She must have thought I was hot on her trail, when truth be told, we were stumped and looking at dead ends all round.'

46

'Lyndsey, darlin'. How's it going? I see in yesterday's local paper that you and your mate are heroes.'

Bob gave her a bear hug and a kiss on the cheek.

'I'm not sure Inspector Savage agrees, but after giving us a dressing down for endangering our lives, he let us go.'

'So Martin and Mary, who would have thought it?'

'Neither admit killing Barry and are blaming each other, so they've both been charged with murder and abducting Mads.'

'How's she doing after her ordeal?'

'She's still upset that her hair won't stop frizzing at the back. You'll be able to ask her yourself in a minute. She came with me but said she had something to sort out. I get scared when she says that because I'm sure it will involve me somehow.'

'Here she comes.'

Lyndsey turned her head as Mads rounded the corner and headed towards them with a big smile on her face.

'Mads, I love what you've done with your hair,' said Bob with a grin.

'Sore point,' she said, pulling her beanie hat down self-consciously.

'I'll go set up my stall while Mads entertains you with her tales of derring-do. I've heard them so often by now, I can almost recite them word for word.'

Lyndsey walked through the mirror path and opened the back doors of the van.

'Here you are, Bob,' said Mads. 'There's the money you lent Barry.'

'No, no. Don't be daft, I don't want your money.'

'It's not. Barry borrowed from everyone because he was being fleeced at poker. This is out of the winnings our friend John won when he went to the same game. So it is your money if you think about it.'

Bob hesitated.

'Take it, buy Jools something nice.'

'You listen to her,' said Jools appearing from nowhere. 'She knows what she's talking about, that one.'

'I swear you were born with bat ears, woman!' said Bob.

'All the better to hear you with, my sweet.'

She kissed him on the cheek and went back to the van. He took the money and put it in his pocket.

'Thanks for that, Lynds doesn't know does she?'

Mads winked. 'Our secret.'

Bob went to help Jools, leaving Mads to walk through the mirrors to Lyndsey's stall.

'What was so important you had to sort it out at six o'clock on a Saturday morning?' asked Lyndsey.

'I made an advance payment on a couple of market stalls.'

Lyndsey raised her eyebrows.

'You? What are you going to be selling?'

'Art. I thought I'd start with Pete and Jen's work and filter mine in as I create it. I've also rented Mary's old studio on the island.'

'You're going to paint again? Oh Mads, I'm so pleased for you. But why do you need two stalls?'

'Well, mine is the one in the corner that Martin and Mary used to share. Then I thought you'd like Barry's old pitch, so I struck a deal with John's dad. You're famous on a local level. Take advantage and start selling murder mysteries. Your old newspaper will lap it up and give you all the publicity you need. It will also give you the rest of the week to write.'

'But ... I haven't got any money to buy stock.'

'Don't you worry about that. I know a few people in the industry, or their wives at least, which is as good as. I'm sure you'll find they'll be only too happy to help. You'd be surprised how being the wife of an investment banker can open doors. No one wants to get on your bad side.'

Mads smiled her mischievous smile.

'But ... but, I don't know what to say.'

'Don't say anything. We're a team. Hey, what about doing children's books? You write the stories and I can illustrate them.'

'Slow down there, Tiger. You've had a couple of days to plan my life for me. At least let me catch up.'

'Well, don't take too long. Our next adventure might be just around the corner.'

'Haven't you had enough excitement for one life-time? You could have been killed.'

'But I wasn't, and together we can do anything we put our minds to. Trust me!'

Lyndsey sighed. If there were two more dangerous words in Mads' vocabulary, she had yet to hear them.

Note from the author

Thank you for reading Must Flea and I hope you enjoyed it. If so, I would very much appreciate a review at Amazon, GoodReads or wherever your preferred book review platform may be.

If you would like to be kept up to date with anything else I am writing, please visit http://www.dsfloyd.com and sign up for my free newsletter.

This book has been checked for errors, but should you find any then please tell me via dave@dsfloyd.com so they can be rectified.

BLOOD READ
A MADS & LYNDSEY MYSTERY

D S FLOYD

Due July 2017

Travel back in time to when Mads & Lyndsey were university students, Lyndsey's part-time library job leads her to discover some mysterious notes threatening the library managers. When no one takes her seriously, she enlists Mads to help find who is responsible.

As managers begin to drop like Autumn leaves, Mads and Lyndsey realise they can't be Dewey-eyed about this library assignment. But will they be able to bring the culprit to book?

ISBN 978-1-898735-03-8